Dorak and the Crystal Caves

Kay Hawkins

Dorak And The Crystal Caves

Published by Starchasers Press

Paperback: 978-1-989548-26-4

Hardcover: 978-1-989548-27-1

Ebook Edition: 978-1-989548-28-8

Front Cover Artist: Chris Nazgul

Back Cover Artist: Albert Bierstadt

Previously Published Stories:

Dorak and the Crystal Caves 2024

Dorak and the Monarchs of Centoria 2024

Dorak on the Road to Kelonia 2024

Dorak at the Gates of Merlienland 2024

Dorak and the Mages College 2024

Dorak and the Archery Contest 2024

Contents

Dedication

To George for inspiring this series

Map

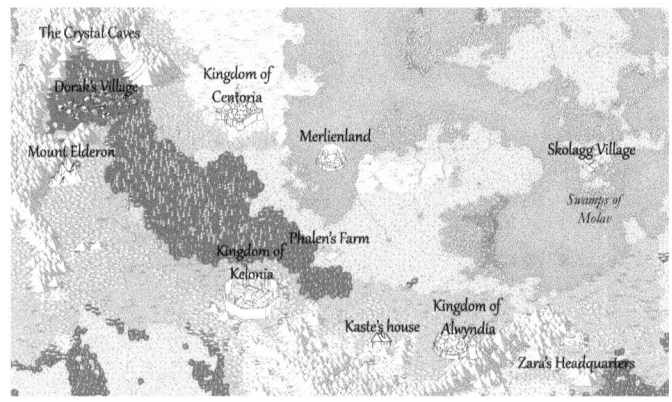

Dorak and the Crystal Caves

Atop the peak above the village, Dorak sat looking over the small area of the world that he knew. He pondered what else lay beyond the familiar sights. As a member of the protectors of the Crystal Caves, his youthful curiosity had often led him to wander farther than advisable, yet his ventures never extended beyond the road to the city once. From his vantage point, everything seemed composed merely of rocks and trees, mirroring the area he had grown up in. However, straining his gaze, he could spot Mount Elderon, where the gods were rumored to reside, the distant canyon, and a few other cities. Despite their allure, he questioned the relevance of such distant places to a barbarian warrior's life, yet the wonder persisted. He found solace and peace in his retreats to this lookout, a place not far from his village but secluded enough to offer solitude. He was nearly lulled to sleep by the tranquility of the tall grass when suddenly, a mass of black clouds gathered, foreboding rain. Yet, as he rose to return to the village, an unusual blue lightning struck the earth. He recognized instantly: this was no ordinary storm, but a display of magical lightning.

Racing down the hill, he witnessed chaos unfold in his village; fire and lightning ravaged the ground. Despite his swift descent, he felt agonizingly distant. Many of the villagers had already fallen when reached the valley floor, breathing their last defiant breaths as two masked strangers atop flying undead steeds pressed the attack from above, hurtling bolts of fire and lightning down on the helpless villagers. Dorak grasped his father's battle axe, launching it at one of the spectral horses. The blade barely grazed the beast's leg, dismounting the wizard with a thud. The sorceress riding alongside him retaliated with a lightning bolt, propelling Dorak through the air with its force. She helped the wizard to his feet and they continued towards their true objective: the Crystal Caves' entrance.

Bruised and disoriented, Dorak realized he lay beside his father's dying form. Tenderly, he placed his hands on his father's shoulders. "Father, please be okay, what is going on?"

His father coughed up some blood and said. "Dorak, my son, the Caves have been lost, and we have failed. Go, run and save yourself; you are the last one."

"But father, our oath, you can't leave me like this."

"You are a strong man. I may not have told you that in the past. I am glad that you are the one who will survive. Their magic is too strong for us; you cannot defeat them like this." His father's words started to fade.

Dorak held his father tightly in those last few moments, then let out a loud cry for the massacre that had happened here today. What was he to do? The caves he was born and sworn to protect had been taken by unknown magical forces, everyone he knew and loved was dead. To leave everything and go where? He looked around and saw the dead, intact body of his best friend Tarkas and grabbed it, throwing it over his shoulder. He picked up his father's battle axe off the ground and headed off into the distance. "If there is nothing that can be done back home, then I will go to the gods and see what they will say."

For days, he carried the body of his best friend through the forest and mountains. The corpse began to rot and smell, but if he was ever going to find peace in this world, he wasn't going to do it alone. He had never been to the top of this mountain or even to the base; this was further than he had ever traveled before. He just knew the gods lived at the top of this mountain, and he would go there to meet them, seeking answers, justice, or perhaps a new purpose in a world that had been turned upside down by tragedy and magic.

When he reached the top of the mountain, there was a large gate that was locked. He reached out, grabbed the lock on the gate, and pulled it off. 'Not protected by magic, odd,' he thought. As he went through the gates, he saw the ruins of an old city with stone paths and buildings. As he walked further in, guards appeared in front of him.

"Stop, how did you get past the gate?"

"Your gate was weak. Now let me through; I need to speak with the gods," he said, attempting to brush their weapons aside.

"Not so fast. Mortals are prohibited here!" one of the guards said.

"I don't care. I have a pressing matter to discuss with them. The Crystal Caves have been taken."

A man walking from one building to the next overheard and approached. "Did you say the Crystal Caves?"

"Yes, I am the last of the protectors of the Caves, and I have come to seek your assistance."

The man saw the rotting corpse of Tarkas and covered his nose. "I'll call a meeting, but ew, what is that disgusting thing?"

"The remains of my best friend and the smartest man the protectors ever knew."

"Mortals are so weird. Follow me." The man led them to a building across the courtyard with a large hall. "Wait here; I will gather the others."

With nowhere around that looked like a suitable chair for a guest, he sat on the stone floor next to the body of his dead friend.

After some time, the gods entered the hall one by one and took their seats. There were eight of them in front of him. A mature, dark-haired one in the center spoke first. "Who are you, and what brings you here?"

"I am Dorak of the protectors of the Crystal Caves, and I have come to inform you of a great new evil force that has taken the Caves. My whole village was wiped out."

"Why do you think this concerns us? We didn't instruct you to protect these caves," the god replied.

Dorak, faced with the indifference of the gods, realized the gravity of his quest. Not only did he need to convince them of the threat but also to appeal to their sense of duty towards the world they overlooked. The loss of the Crystal Caves was not just a local tragedy but a sign of a burgeoning darkness that could threaten the balance of power and the very essence of magic they all depended on.

"Sir, if these magic users took the caves, they wield great power. They could come here and to countless other places in the world. They are out to kill and destroy the world!" he shouted.

"Let them. What goes on anywhere else but here is none of our business. We are protected and can handle ourselves." He waved his hand dismissively. "Leave this place and take the corpse of your friend with you; it is unpleasant." They all got up and began to leave.

"I was taught to look up to you! You were supposed to be all-knowing and powerful!"

The dark-haired one turned around. "It doesn't mean we help people."

The hall went dark, and Dorak stood there in the hall alone, with his friend once again, disappointed with the results. Was there nothing he could do?

A little while later, a lady with long blonde hair came back into the room. "Do you still wish for assistance?"

He looked up into her calm, pale eyes. "I have nothing left."

She held out her hand. "Come with me, then, and I will help you and your friend."

He followed her through the back of the building to a lovely court-yard with a gigantic tree and a fountain surrounded by lush green vines.

"What is this place?" he asked.

"The Fountain of Life. It is what gave us gods our powers. It is the reason we are here to protect it. A long time ago, this was our village, and it was full of people. We all drank from this fountain. For some, it granted magic; for others, it granted eternal life; and others it cursed with diseases, and they died. The survivors, including me, vowed to protect it and never let anyone drink from this fountain again because its effects are unpredictable. I want you to give some of the water to your friend."

"Why are you helping me? Why, after all this time, do you trust me?" He carried his friend to the fountain.

"Because I know of the magic in this world, and you are right to be concerned about them. We will need someone to protect us, and because you are from the Crystal Caves, the water is very similar in power. Also, your friend is already dead; I can't see why it would hurt them to drink of the waters."

Dorak cupped some of the water in his hand and placed it into his friend's mouth. While he waited for something to happen, he asked. "Who are you? And why are you helping and not the others?"

"I am Wella, and the man in there was Caspher. He is jaded by the events of the past, and we gods have been around so long that some of us want to die. But no ordinary person is supposed to be able to break our locks; those are warded by magic. Maybe that has to do with your gift of strength from the Crystal Caves."

"Well, someone did, and if I could, the wizard and the sorceress can too. You need to up the security here because if they went after the caves, they will come here eventually."

She walked over to the large tree and tapped the side of it. "We will be prepared for that." A bright light emanated from the tree, and a door opened up. She pulled out a red-bladed battle-axe and a red bow. "This is the Tree of Life, as we call it, and it gets its power from the fountain's waters." She took the weapons over to Dorak and his friend, handing them to Dorak.

"What is this?" he asked.

"This is a petrified axe enchanted by magic. Take this the weapon and defeat that wizard. You will need it." She looked over at his friend lying there still, then touched his face, and new breath came into his body.

"Where am I?" his friend said.

"You are in the Garden of the Gods, in the kingdom of the gods. Your friend Dorak saved your life." She handed him the bow. "You're an archer, right?"

He nodded his head and took the bow. He looked over at his friend and said. "Really, you saved me, but what about your father?"

Dorak looked down at his friend and let out a single tear. "Your body was the only one intact, and if I was going to fight the forces of darkness, I wanted it to be by your side, my friend."

His friend gave him a hug and looked at the gash on his arm. "Well, I don't know how intact I am."

"Let's see if you can stand," Wella said, holding out her hand.

Dorak and Wella helped him up; there was a bit of a struggle with the decaying muscles. "I'm not going to look like a zombie forever, am I?"

"I'm sure a lot of it will heal over time. You were dead for a week, right?" Wella said, looking at Dorak.

He nodded. "We are far from our village, or what is left of it. The sorceress wiped us out and took the Caves. I'll fill you in on the way to..." he stopped. "what are we doing after this?"

Wella smiled. "You are going to set out on a quest to defeat these new forces of evil, in whatever way suits you. But you will stop them from achieving their goal by protecting the innocent."

Dorak smiled. "That sounds like a good plan."

Wella went over to the fountain and filled up a canteen, then handed it to Tarkas. "Take this and only drink it if you feel ill. I have no idea how much time the fountain has given you. Please stay safe, you two, and I believe in you."

Dorak attached his axe to his belt. "You have my word, thank you for all of this."

Wella's head turned when they all heard a noise. "That is Caspher. Quickly follow me; I will get you out of here. He must not know what I have given you two. Please follow me now and be quiet."

They followed her through the run-down stone streets of the city to a much older overgrown gate. She opened it with her key. "Go out this way and be prosperous in your journey. Also, don't come back here; you will not be welcomed."

They snuck out the gate and ran down the path. Dorak looked one more time back at Wella to see she blew him a kiss before locking the gate.

Dorak and Tarkas ran down the path of the mountain. When they were closer to the base, Dorak looked around. "Which way do you think Centoria city is?"

Tarkas pointed to the southeast. "I looked as we were climbing down the mountain. By the way, why do you want to go there?"

"Well, we have to tell them that the caves have been taken and that we have failed our duty. I'll show them my father's battle axe as proof." He pointed to the axe he was carrying on his back. "Unless you think they attacked the city?"

Tarkas shook his head. "No, they were after power and magic. They wanted the crystals."

"Then it's off to Centoria city," Dorak said as they began the next step of their journey.

Dorak and the Monarchs of Centoria

On their way to Centoria City, Tarkas turned to Dorak and said, "since we are heading back, should we stop by the village and bury the dead?"

Dorak was silent for a moment. "Under any other circumstances, I would say yes, we should, but we don't know what the evil duo has done, and there is no time to waste. We can't build a mound. Let our fallen families be a gift to the beasts."

Tarkas nodded. "Understood."

It was longer to the city than they had planned. From the village to the mountain pass, it was around 7 days, but because they were avoiding the village, it added an extra 3 days to their trip. However, they were used to living outdoors, and this quest was just another passage of time. Tarkas fashioned new arrows from the branches of trees that he found and used them to hunt and kill small beasts for them to eat. Dorak would cut and clean the beasts. One night by the campfire, Dorak said to Tarkas, "maybe we could catch one of these wild beasts and tame it to ride, and then we will have a faster way of getting around?"

Tarkas finished his bite of hare leg. "I think that we are best to wait until the city. While that is a good idea, we would have better luck with an already tame beast. We should be there by tomorrow evening."

They finished their food and went to sleep. In the morning, they continued their journey to Centoria. As soon as they got to the city, swarms of women rushed to them. Tarkas raised his hand to brush some of the ladies aside. "Ladies, we are not here seeking wives. We need to speak to the king."

Dorak admired some of the ladies that came up to him but tried to stay focused until a mother approached with her stubborn daughter. "Please, protector of the Crystal Caves, marry my daughter. She is too stubborn, and no man will marry her. She would make a great barbarian wife."

The fiery redhead snapped back at her mother. "I don't want to get married, ugh! Stop trying to set me up with everyone."

Dorak stopped in his tracks and addressed the mother. "While I think you are right, I have to tell you that I'm not here looking for a wife. I know it is tradition when a protector of the Caves comes to the city they are looking for a wife, but there are no more protectors. We have come to tell the king that evil magical forces have wiped us out."

Tarkas came over. "Don't say anything like that. We have to tell the king first."

The villagers were shocked, trying to ask more questions. Tarkas waved his hand dismissively. "No questions. We have to get to the king before it is too late."

"Please take my daughter anyway; she is strong. She could be useful," the pushy mother said.

Dorak shook his head. "She seems like a fine lady, but official business first."

They walked away and made their way to the castle. It was dark, and the king was in bed, but his man-at-arms went and got him when he heard of the urgency.

Dorak and Tarkas sat in the food hall waiting for the king. The young prince came running out to see the men. The young prince, no older than ten, sat next to Dorak, "Are you one of the protectors of the Crystal Caves?"

Dorak finished his bite of venison. "Why, yes, I am Dorak, and this is my friend Tarkas. What might your name be, little prince?"

"I am Prince Eldrin. I'm third in line to the throne. Is it true that you are super strong?"

"Stand up and grab my arm, and I will show you." Dorak got up and held out his arm for the kid to grab, then he started lifting the kid with one arm. "Is that strong to you?" He let the prince down.

"Yeah, that is super strong!"

"Ahem," said the king as he entered the food hall. "What is this matter that is so important you must wake the king at this hour?"

Tarkas got up, and he and Dorak both got on one knee. "Your Highness, we bring sad news from the Crystal Caves." Dorak took his father's battle axe off his back and presented it to the king. "King Alaric, my father Gorak, who was, as you know, the leader of the protectors of the Crystal Caves, is dead, and so is the right of our village. Me and Tarkas are all that survive. We have failed to protect the caves from an evil wizard and sorceress. We are sorry, Your Majesty, but we have failed in our duty, and the caves have fallen to the powers of darkness."

The king stood silent and stared at the battle axe. He examined it closely. "I remember this axe; I was the king who gave it to him. I'm sorry that your people have fallen. What do you request of me now?"

Tarkas spoke up. "We wish to avenge our fallen families and pursue the evil duo and attack them. We have been granted magical weapons by the gods, but we need an army, some warriors, to go and pursue them. They are going after the magical places in the world, building power. The cave may no longer be ours, but we can fight back."

"No, you cannot have my warriors. You failed at your job and now want to weaken my city? Absolutely not! You can live in the city because you are citizens, but no, we need our defenses up now!" King Alaric said.

Tarkas spoke up. "Sir, please reconsider."

The king turned to his man-at-arms. "Make up a room for them in the barracks."

"Right away—" before the man-at-arms could finish what he was saying, a blue-skinned elf appeared and spoke up. "Father, let me go with them."

Dorak and Tarkas were shocked; it had been a long time since one of them had seen an elf.

"Kal, go back to bed. You are not going anywhere, especially with them. You are my son," the king said.

"I am your bastard son and not your heir. I'm an elf; there is no future for me here, and I know where the sorceress might be going. They will probably be attacking Kelonia City where my cousin lives," Kal said.

The king shuddered at the mention of the cousin. "You are my son and prince here in these city walls. If you leave, you have no protection. We need you here with the army."

"You might have loved my mother, but you have two other sons by your wife. There are no other elves in this kingdom. I don't care if I'm a prince here; it means nothing. The forces of evil are serious and need to be taken care of. We don't have the magic to protect us if they attack. These heroes need to go out and fight it at its source and protect others. I've got no future here, and you know that, always trying to deny it. Give these men the resources they need and let me go with them," Kal shouted.

"Calm down and do not speak to your father and king like that!" he snapped back. He paused for a moment and then said, ";et me think about it. We will all get some sleep and talk about it tomorrow."

Tarkas wanted to say something, but with the king tired, there was no progress that was going to be made tonight. The man-at-arms showed them to their room where they would sleep.

In the royal hall, Kal was packing his bags. His brother Prince Joren came over when he heard the ruckus.

"Kal, why are you packing?" Joren said.

He turned to his brother. "Because I'm leaving for good and for a higher purpose."

Joren placed his hand on his brother's, stopping him from packing. "What? You can't leave; you're my brother. What am I going to do without you?"

Kal sat down on the bed and looked up at his brother. "You don't understand what it's like to be me. I'm the only one of my kind, your mother hates me. Dad likes me, but I'm a bastard prince; no one will marry me here, and I don't fit in. I'm a good military commander because I have put all my efforts into it. But there is an evil duo who alone took the Crystal Caves. I have heard about the kingdom of

Kelonia that guards a magic relic, and my mother's family is there. I need to look them up and find out more about who I am."

Prince Joren stared down at his brother. "You are second in line to the throne; you are needed here in case I'm away or something happens. Bro, I thought we were best friends."

He stood up and gave Kal a hug. "We are, and nothing is going to change that." He broke the hug. "But we are different people. You still have me, and yeah, about that, I'm second in line but only because you're human. I'm older than you; ask dad. So if something happens to you, Eldrin is the one. There is no point in me staying."

"You are my only friend; please don't leave me," Joren pleaded.

Kal took a deep breath. "You will be married soon and be starting your own family. I'm not leaving forever. I will come back and see you with your son, I promise."

"If you can convince dad to let you leave, then you better come back. I will wait for you." Joren gave his brother a hug.

In the afternoon, the king awoke and met with the warriors in the main hall. "After you interrupted my sleep last night, I have thought about what to do with you two." The king snapped his fingers, and the man-at-arms came out with an array of weapons. "If you wish to leave and pursue these evil doers, then you may have whatever you need. But the offer also stands that you can live in the city as part of the military. This city will need its defenses for when they come back."

Tarkas spoke up. "Your Highness, these evil doers are after magic. They will not attack here until they have all the magic. You will have time."

"I hope you are right," the king let out a sigh. "So, I guess this means that you are set on your goal to leave."

Dorak stood up. "Your Highness, my whole life was in those caves. I cannot rest until the spirits of my ancestors and family have been avenged. When this is over, I would gladly take you up on this offer, but until then, I have to do all in my power."

"That is understandable, and I can respect that, and I will do my best to honour that," the king said.

As the king finished talking, his son Kal came out with full armor on and a backpack on his back. "I am going with them."

The king glared at his son. "No, you're not, and go to your room!"

"I am not a child anymore. The wizards are going to want to go after the temple at Kelonia, and these two have no idea how to get there or know anyone. I have a cousin, and I want to know about my people. Let me do this and be known for something besides Kal the bastard. Let me fight for our people," Kal snapped back at his father.

The queen, who was at his side, answered. "Let the boy go. He is just taking up space here. Maybe he will be of more use to these barbarians."

The king shot a glare at his wife, then got up and went over to his son and placed his hand on his shoulder. "I never wanted to lose you. Please reconsider; you mean so much to me."

Kal, with a heavy heart, placed his hand on his father's. "This is my destiny. I feel it. I know you loved my mother, but I cannot be kept here anymore. I'm not a child."

The king gave his son a big hug, and with tears forming in his eyes, said. "You can go."

Kal broke the hug and went over to the heroes. Dorak spoke up. "Excuse me, but you look a little small. What qualifies you to work with us?"

Kal shot him a look. "I may not be as large as a man who lives in the wild and was blessed by the cave waters, but I am arguably the strongest soldier my father has, and I'm limber and a cunning hunter and guide. Also, Kelonia City is an elven city; you will need me to talk to them."

Dorak and Tarkas shared a look before nodding in agreement. "You can come with us," Tarkas said.

Kal stood next to his new friends, and they bowed down to King Alaric before leaving the palace.

They walked out of the palace and were heading on the road out of town. "We are not done here yet; we need to go to the stables," Kal said. "I wouldn't leave without my horse."

They made their way to the stables. The stable master took one look at Dorak. "I'm sorry, sir, but I have no horse that can carry you. Maybe your friend, but as much as I support your work, I cannot provide you a horse."

Kal spoke up. "Well, I will be needing my horse. But do you not have another beast of burden that could carry these men?"

The stable master shook his head. "I can get your horse, but I have nothing for them; they are too large. But as for other beasts, I have heard of a stable that is on the way to Kelonia city that has unique creatures; maybe they have something there."

Dorak turned to Tarkas in agreement. "That is the way we are headed; we can go there."

Kal took his horse from the stable boy and brushed the nose of the horse, giving it a gentle hug. He turned to the others. "I'm ready to go, are you?"

They all made their way out of the city with Kal leading his horse. They were just at the city's edge when a woman in a blue dress came running over to them with a man-at-arms. "Wait, stop," she called.

Dorak recognized the woman from the day before; she was the one whose mother tried to marry him off to her. The man-at-arms went over to Kal and handed him a medallion. "Your father wanted you to have this."

Kal examined the medallion; it was the royal seal. As much as he was renouncing his place in the royal line, this was a symbol that his father still considered him a part of the family and that he could come home one day. "Thank you," he said, taking the medallion and placing it in his bag.

The woman went up to Dorak. "My name is Lira, and I want to come with you."

Dorak waved his hand. "No, I'm not looking for a wife; it is too dangerous."

She snapped back. "I don't want a husband; I want to get out of this place. It's too small, and I'd rather be fighting the forces of evil than spend another season listening to my mother and farming. Please take me with you!"

Tarkas responded. "Alright, what skills do you have?"

"I can cook, repair armor, and I have some sword-fighting skills, I will learn. Please take me with you. I could carry your armor." She pleaded.

Kal spoke up. "Lira, you are not allowed to leave the city as a citizen without the king's approval. It would have been okay if you had married Dorak because he is from one of the tribes outside, but we have a duty to keep the population up. But in this case, I can approve you coming with us if those two agree." He stared at the others.

Dorak thought about it for a long moment. "You can come, but you need to carry your own weight. Right now, any help against these evil doers is needed."

They all shared a look of agreement with each other, then Kal said to the man-at-arms. "Go tell my father that the maiden Lira is coming with us, by my order."

The man nodded. "Yes, Your Highness." He bowed and headed back toward the road ahead.

"Now, will there be any more interruptions?" Dorak asked.

"I do not expect so," Kal answered.

"Then let's not waste any more time." They all began on their next journey northeast to the kingdom of Kelonia, with Kal as their guide to the city, hoping they would get there before the forces of evil did.

Dorak on the road to Kelonia

"How much further to the stables?" Lira asked, her voice laced with a mix of anticipation and fatigue.

Tarkas gazed thoughtfully at the sky before responding. "I would say about one more day. It won't be much longer after that until we get to Kelonia City. I think they are two days from there, but if we all have beasts, it should be quicker." He turned his attention to Lira, a hint of concern in his tone. "Are your feet tired?"

She shook her head, a determined spark in her eyes. "No, I'm just not used to sleeping outside this much."

Kal laughed softly. "I understand what you mean. I've done it, but I will say it's an adjustment."

"Would you two stop complaining? You both chose to come on this journey," Dorak interjected, his voice carrying the weight of their shared burdens.

"I was just saying it was an adjustment. I'm not complaining; I am excited for this journey," Lira clarified, her spirit undiminished by the hardships.

"After what I have seen, how can anyone be excited for what we are expected to face?" Dorak mused, his gaze fixed on the path ahead, betraying a sense of solemn responsibility.

Tarkas spoke up, attempting to soothe the growing tension. "Sorry, this has been a rough time for us. Don't take it personally. We are glad to have your help."

That night, as they made camp, Kal ventured out and returned with a wild boar, its size testament to his skill as a hunter.

Dorak eyed the size of the beast with a mix of surprise and pragmatism. "It's a bit large for us to eat in one sitting."

"We can salt some of it and take it with us. I was thinking ahead. Why, do you have something against me for providing?" Kal retorted, his frustration flaring at the perceived slight.

"You're some fancy prince showing off, thinking this is some fun adventure. Do you not realize these evil doers are heartless murderers who wield magic? What magic do you have?" Dorak challenged, his concern for their mission outweighing his patience.

"I don't know. I know nothing about my elven heritage. And I want to. I was raised by humans and confined to a palace against my will. I need to discover who I am. If there's a chance I can be something more, I'll find out and take the risk," Kal shot back.

Lira, returning from lookout duty, rushed back to the camp with urgent news. "Guys, we need to be cautious. I think the wizard you speak of is not too far away."

Kal acted swiftly, dousing the fire with ashes to minimize their visibility. They all followed Lira to the lookout spot, where a distant fire pit was visible. Kal scaled a tall tree for a better view. After a few moments, he returned, confirming their fears. "Definitely, a small group of magic wielders. They weren't wearing their skull masks, just sitting around the campfire."

"Skull masks, that's them," Dorak said, his hand instinctively reaching for his red battle-axe. "How many are there?"

"I only saw four, but there could be more," Kal replied, the uncertainty in his voice hinting at the dangers of their potential adversaries.

"Well, I'm not letting them get away," Dorak declared, sword in hand, ready to move forward. "Let's go get them."

Tarkas placed a reassuring hand on Dorak's shoulder, urging caution. "Let's not. They are still more powerful, and what if it's not them?"

Dorak's glare at Tarkas was fierce, yet it revealed his deep-seated resolve. "We can take them now while they're weak and not expecting it," he argued, ready to confront their foes despite the risks.

Tarkas, refusing to let go of his friend, proposed a cautious approach. "Let's wait until they are asleep and explore the camp. Kal and I can go in stealth, but we need to find out their plans and be one step ahead."

Dorak's anger subsided, acknowledging the wisdom in Tarkas's suggestion. "You were always the smart one. Go and find out what you can."

The group unanimously decided to split; Dorak and Lira would stay at their camp while Kal and Tarkas ventured to the enemy camp. Hiding in the nearby bushes, they waited until their foes had retired for the night. Tarkas was puzzled by the lack of a lookout, despite the small number of their adversaries, but proceeded with caution.

"If they are asleep, we should slit their throats and save ourselves the trouble," Kal whispered.

"They are magic users; they probably have wards protecting them," Tarkas countered, moving closer. Once he was sure the lookout had also fallen asleep, they split up, Kal heading towards the sorceress while Tarkas approached the wizard. Tarkas could only get a vague view of a dark-haired man by the campfire, but something about him seemed familiar. Drawing closer, he realized the man resembled someone from the protectors of the Crystal Caves, believed to have died years ago. Doubt crept into his mind as he spotted the ornate skull staff lying unprotected next to the sleeping figure. Tentatively, Tarkas reached for the staff, only for the wizard's eyes to snap open, locking gazes with him. The recognition was immediate when Tarkas saw the green eyes; it was indeed the man he knew, confirming his betrayal.

The man's hand shot out, gripping Tarkas's wrist. "Drop the staff."

In shock, Tarkas released the staff, and the wizard released him, pretending to sleep again. Realizing his fortunate escape, Tarkas decided not to push his luck further. Glancing at Kal, who was inches away from the sorceress with his knife drawn, Tarkas felt a surge of anxiety. Unable to proceed, Kal found an invisible force field blocking his path. Signaling to retreat, Tarkas and Kal hastily made their way back to their own camp.

Upon their return, they found Dorak and Lira asleep. Kal, contemplating their next move, asked. "Should we wake them?"

Tarkas, observing the moon's position, concluded they needed rest for the challenges ahead. "No, they probably fell asleep waiting for us, and after what we overheard, we're going to need the rest for the long journey tomorrow."

They settled down beside their companions, waiting for dawn.

When morning arrived, an eager Dorak roused them. "So, what's the report?"

Tarkas hesitated, unsure whether to reveal the identity of the wizard in front of everyone. "It was them, and we were right about their plan to attack the temple."

Kal revealed a large red carved stone from his bag. "I stole this from one of their companions. I don't know what it means, but I managed to take it."

Tarkas's eyes widened in disbelief. "You stole from them!"

"Excuse me, but did I not see you try to take the wizard's staff?" Kal retorted.

He sighed. "I did, and it turns out it was protected. My guess is if you could steal that, the magic of the others is not as strong as theirs," Tarkas said.

Dorak took the carved stone from Kal and examined it closely, his brow furrowing. "I've never seen anything like it."

Lira leaned in to get a better look while Dorak held it. "It's magic of some sort. Look at this writing; it isn't from around here."

Nonchalantly, Dorak tossed it in the air, catching it again with ease. "Whatever it is, someone hold onto it and don't lose it."

Tarkas grabbed the stone and secured it in his pouch. "We need to get moving. We're not far from the stables. We'll get something there and try to rush to the city by the end of today if we're going to beat them to the city."

"I could ride ahead on my horse if that will help?" Kal suggested, eager to contribute.

"No need. We will be there soon. But I think we need to get going; we can eat on the way," Tarkas urged.

They set off as a team towards their next destination: the stables. Arriving in good time, they observed from the outside a stable of unusual beasts. With no one in sight, Dorak approached the door of a small log cabin and knocked. A man opened the door, eyeing Dorak from head to toe before declaring. "I got just the beast for you."

He led them all to the back of the yard, where they were greeted by an array of extraordinary creatures. The man guided them to the gryphon stables. "These beasts of burden will support a man of your size. They were bred and raised by me and are fully domesticated. Is it just for you, or do your friends need one?"

"It would be nice to get one for me, Tarkas, and Lira, if we could," Dorak said, hopeful.

"That will cost a lot of money," the man warned. "But I can equip your team with what you need, if you have the coin."

Dorak, unfamiliar with dealing in currency, turned back to his group. "Does anyone have currency?"

Kal produced a bag of coins and handed them to the man. "Are these acceptable here?"

The man examined the bag, his expression unimpressed. "It is not enough for one beast, unless you are willing to trade in your royal steed."

Kal, taken aback, protested. "Why would you want my horse!"

"The royal horses come from a very uncommon bloodline that I would love to breed with mine. But I have to be able to purchase one."

"Gabe, my horse has been mine since I was a child. I couldn't give him up regardless," Kal stated firmly.

"It's a male, you say?" the stable master inquired, intrigued.

Kal, puzzled, asked. "What does that have to do with anything?"

"You don't have to sell me your horse; you just need to leave it with me for a few days. I can use it for breeding, and if I get at least one foal from that, it will be worth more than four of the gryphons."

Kal fell silent, contemplating the offer. Tarkas, seeing his friend's hesitation, spoke up. "While my friend thinks about it, I want to mention that we are on a time crunch to get to Kelonia City. Is there a way that we could maybe just make this deal quickly?"

"A gryphon can carry two of you and will get you to the city in under two hours, so we have some time. How long do you plan to stay in Kelonia?" the man asked.

"We are trying to stop an attack, so we need to get there soon. We don't have a set time of how long we will be there," Tarkas explained.

Kal, seizing the moment, negotiated. "I will leave you my horse, but you must provide us with two gryphons to get us to the city."

The man pondered for a brief moment before agreeing. "You've got yourself a deal." With that, Kal and the stable master sealed the agreement with a handshake.

The stable master then showed Tarkas and Dorak the gryphons and explained how to ride them. Meanwhile, Lira, curious about the arrangement, questioned Kal. "Did you know this about the royal horses?"

Kal, somewhat detached from the intricacies of royal customs, replied. "I knew they were bred for the royal family but not much more than that. I'm not into husbandry."

"Are you supposed to breed your horse without royal permission?" Lira probed further.

"No one ever mentioned anything about it to me. Also, I'm no longer a prince. The fact that they let me keep my horse when I left suggests they can't care too much about it," Kal reasoned.

After Tarkas and Dorak were briefed on the gryphons, the stable master turned his attention to Kal's horse, expressing interest in examining the steed.

At the front of the stable, Kal's majestic white horse, adorned in the brown and green armor of his kingdom, caught everyone's eye. Speaking softly to his horse, Kal reassured. "Hey, buddy, I'm going to leave you here for a few days. This man will take good care of you, and you're going to have a good time, alright? I'll come back for you," as he affectionately petted its nose.

"What's the steed's name?" inquired the stable master.

After a brief pause, Kal responded. "Gabe; that was the name the stables gave him. He was a gift to me on my tenth birthday from my father. Please take good care of him."

The stable master assured. "He will be in good hands."

Rejoining his companions, already mounted on the gryphons and ready to depart, Kal found Lira riding behind Dorak. Tarkas called out. "Come on! We're ready to go."

Kal climbed up behind Tarkas, and soon they were soaring into the sky. The experience of flying above the trees, seeing the landscape stretch out below them, was awe-inspiring. Tarkas pointed out their destination. "There, that walled city, is Kelonia."

As they flew, Lira scanned the ground below, searching for any sign of the evil troupe. "I don't see them. Don't you think we would see them traveling if we are this high up?"

Dorak, struggling with motion sickness, managed to say, "I would assume they have magic that can hide their movements."

Upon landing, Dorak rushed to find a spot to relieve his nausea, affirming. "I much prefer staying on the ground."

They proceeded to the stables outside the city, where Kal arranged for their gryphons to be cared for. Approaching the city gates, he reassured Tarkas. "I'll handle everything when we get to the gates. They are well guarded."

As anticipated, the guards halted their approach. Kal stepped forward confidently. "I am Prince Kal, son of King Alaric and Lady Karina. I have family in the city and wish to visit them with my friends."

The guards looked him over and nodded their heads. "We can tell by your armor who you are and your friends are free to visit the city." They opened the gates, and the group walked in.

Once inside the city walls, Kal's heart swelled with joy at the sight of a city full of people with blue skin like his own. He felt an overwhelming sense of happiness, finally seeing the city his family called home.

Tarkas was captivated by the white stone buildings that filled the city. It was clean, bright, and utterly foreign to him, unlike anything he had seen before. "So, where to, Kal?"

Kal snapped out of his reverie. "I'm not sure where my cousin could be, so I guess we need to head to the palace first." They walked through the city, past all the shops in the marketplace where vendors were selling elven goods, jewelry, clothes, and food. Tarkas looked back. "We will stop to shop when we have finished our mission."

They made it to the palace. The guards stopped them again. Kal addressed them. "I am Prince Kal of Centoria. I need to speak with the queen about the danger of an evil wizard and sorceress after the magic in the Temple of Kelonia."

The guard narrowed his eyes, skeptical. "How do you know about this attack? Is this a trap? Your father tried to invade us years ago."

Tarkas intervened. "Me and my friend Dorak are all that remain of the protectors of the Crystal Caves. They have fallen to the hands of an evil wizard and sorceress. King Alaric had nothing to do with this."

"You look like a prince, and I will let you in, but you will need to convince the queen," the guard conceded.

Inside the palace, the elven queen sat on her throne, dressed in a white and blue gown. Atop her white hair, she wore a crown with blue crystal spheres. She gave a sly grin upon seeing Kal. "So, Prince Kal, your father has finally given you freedom and allowed you to come live among your people."

Kal and the group bowed to the queen. "Your Majesty, I left of my own free will. And I am surprised that you know so much about me."

"You and your friends don't need to bow. And I know so much about you because you are the only Elven prince outside of this city," she stated.

"Well, I have renounced my claim to the throne because my father was never going to recognize me as his heir. But enough about that, I need to talk to you about a more pressing matter. There is going to be an attack on the temple very soon," Kal said, gesturing to Dorak. "My friend Dorak will tell you."

Dorak stepped forward. "Your Majesty, I am Dorak son of Gorak, the former leader of the Crystal Caves. I witnessed my village being wiped out by an evil wizard and sorceress, and on our way here, we saw that they are coming this way, seeking the power in your temple."

The queen paused thoughtfully. "Why do you know so much about them?"

"Because I have lived through their devastation, and I have sought counsel with the gods," Dorak explained. He pulled out his red battle-axe and showed it to her. "This was a gift from the gods to fight these evildoers. I do not want what happened to my people to happen to yours."

The queen summoned her mage. "Do you know if there's any truth to what these people are saying?"

The mage, a female elf with long black hair, dressed in a dark brown robe, examined the battle-axe carefully. "I believe he is telling the truth, Your Majesty. This battle-axe holds ancient powers, and I did feel a few weeks ago a disturbance in the balance of magic. We must protect the temple."

"Well, it would appear you have arrived just in time. You may go to the food hall and enjoy yourselves. After you eat, we will convene at the temple. You are all guests of the queen now, and you will be given quarters," the queen declared. She gestured to one of the guards. "Give them a tour of the palace."

Kal, seizing the opportunity, inquired. "Your Majesty, where might I find my cousin or other family I may have left?"

"Your cousin can be found in the armory; she is one of our top knights. She may be helpful to you," Queen Keltrice said.

Following the guard's lead, they toured the palace, were shown to their rooms, and then directed to the food hall. Amidst the meal, Kal, eager to reconnect with his roots, announced, "I'm going to try and find my cousin before we head to the temple."

Lira stood up, joining him. "Let me come with you. I would love to see more of this place."

They made their way to the barracks, where Kal inquired about his cousin. Directed to the end of the hall, Kal approached a woman donned in white and gold armor. "Kaley, is that you?" He asked with a smile.

She turned, her face lighting up with recognition. "Kal, is that you? Wow, you have grown."

After their reunion and introductions, Kal explained. "And this is Lira, one of the people traveling with us, trying to stop the forces of evil. But I have left the royals and hope to spend some time here getting in touch with my roots."

"That's great! I'd be glad to help you with that and offer your friend some training. I assume that's why she came down here," Kaley responded, turning to Lira with a welcoming smile.

"Yeah, when I heard you were a knight, I thought maybe there was a chance for some training. I don't have the skills the men do yet in the group. I want to be better," Lira said, enthusiasm evident in her voice.

"That can be arranged," his cousin assured them, then she equipped her with a sword, emphasizing the impending need at the temple.

Together, they made their way to the Temple of Kelonia, where they reunited with Dorak, Tarkas, and the palace mage. Kal introduced his cousin to the group, sparking curiosity.

Tarkas, intrigued, asked. "Not to intrude, but how is she your cousin? Are there other family members?"

Kal's cousin clarified. "Kal's mother fell in love with the king before he invaded Kelonia. He lost, but because he had an elven son, he thought he had a claim to our throne. After the loss and Kal's mother's passing when he was young, I remained. Our mothers were sisters. My mother tried to persuade her sister to leave the king and return, but she refused. So, the elves dislike King Alaric, and we always hoped Kal would return to his true home. Unfortunately, the rest of our family perished in the battle." Kal, reflecting on his unexpected journey back to his roots, nodded in acknowledgment of his cousin's achievements. "Well, that and I have worked my way up to being one of the captains of the guards. So, if anything threatens my home and people, I'm there to defend it," his cousin, Kaley, stated with pride.

Dorak, grunted in approval. "Good, we will need all the help we can get."

The air thickened with tension as the mage, sensing an imminent threat, announced. "I feel a great disturbance coming near us. I'm not sure how far they are, but it's getting closer."

Dorak, taking immediate command, shouted. "Battle positions!"

Lira, confused about their strategy, voiced her concern. "Where do we stand? You didn't give us a plan."

"Right," Dorak quickly realized his oversight and strategized on the spot. "Let's have the magic users right near the Stone of Kelonia, and we'll form a perimeter around them. How many did you say there were, Tarkas?"

Tarkas, scanning the surroundings, estimated. "About five. They've got three more since they attacked us. One, I think, is an elf."

"An elf, you say?" the mage pondered, connecting the dots. "That would explain what happened to Kellwyn; he disappeared about a month ago. We are going to need to pull out all the stops."

Tarkas, hoping to contribute further, retrieved the red stone from his side pouch. "Will this be of any help?"

After examining the stone, the mage responded. "No, this is not our kind of magic. It's from a different land, I believe to the south of here. When the fight is over, I'll take a closer look."

With the stone safely back in Tarkas's bag, they readied themselves, weapons in hand, awaiting the attack.

Lira, filled with a mix of anticipation and anxiety, suggested. "Should we, like, say anything or talk while we wait?"

"Shush!" Dorak snapped, his focus razor-sharp, as they stood in silence, preparing for the impending confrontation. The air was charged with an uneasy stillness, each of them ready to spring into action at the first sign of the enemy. The weight of their task was palpable; they were not just fighting for themselves but for the protection of Kelonia and the balance of magic itself. They stood there in silence, waiting for the attack. Moments stretched into an eternity until the mage among them clutched her head in agony, falling to her knees. "Ah, they are close! The power, so strong," she gasped.

All eyes turned to her just as a loud crash echoed through the temple. The sorceress, using her dark magic, blew off the roof of the temple. Tarkas, quick to react, fired his arrow at the sorceress, hitting her undead steed. The horse flinched but she maintained her grip. Unfazed, he continued to shoot arrows at her.

The mages present initiated a protective measure, a brain blocker, to shield their minds from being overwhelmed by the sorceress's powerful psychic attacks. Despite their efforts, the sorceress retaliated with lightning bolts, aiming them with deadly precision.

Dorak, not to be outdone, hurled the red axe with all his might at the sorceress, then dashed after Tarkas to provide support. Their focus on the sorceress left an opening, and Kal noticed an elf trying to stealthily take the orb central to the temple's power. He engaged the elf with his sword, but the magical prowess of the elf proved overpowering against the mere steel of Kal's weapon.

Meanwhile, Lira and Kal's cousin Kaley faced off against the other two minions of darkness.

In the midst of the chaos, Tarkas regained his senses and, with a well-aimed shot, wounded the sorceress, momentarily halting her advance. Dorak, seizing the opportunity, engaged in close combat with one of the sorceress's allies. His sword, enchanted to cut through magic, neutralized the enemy's spells, preventing further magical assaults.

Kal, though wounded, persisted in his fight. But as the orb was taken, the elf vanished into thin air, leaving a palpable void where his presence once was. With the orb gone, the villains found their advantage waning and began to retreat.

In a desperate move, the sorceress, noticing Tarkas possessed the red stone, kidnapped him in a whirlwind of dark energy and vanished. The battlefield quieted down, leaving the heroes to grasp the gravity of their situation: Tarkas was gone, and with him, a crucial piece of their fight against the encroaching darkness.

Kal saw them try to leave with Tarkas and shot an arrow at the sorceress without hitting Tarkas and missed. He did manage to hit the evil wizard in the leg but it was no use in getting their friend back.

Dorak's anguished cry echoed through the area as his friend was abducted, leaving him feeling powerless. Meanwhile, Lira showcased her quick reflexes by subduing a man with gills, pinning him to the ground with her sword poised at his throat. "Tell me where they've taken him!" she demanded, her voice firm and authoritative.

The gilled-man, defiant even in his vulnerable position, retorted. "I won't tell you anything."

Dorak, fueled by a mix of worry and anger, rushed to the scene, commanding. "Get up! Both of you!" His voice boomed across the clearing.

As they complied, Dorak instinctively seized the gilled-man by the collar, his voice thundering. "Where have they taken my friend?!"

Met with silence, Dorak's frustration boiled over. "I'm not merely asking—I demand to know where they have gone!"

Trembling with fear under Dorak's intimidating presence, the gill-man finally relented. "They are heading to my world next, the underwater kingdom of Merlienland. They will not return to their base for a long time."

Dorak's response was a fierce growl. "You are going to guide us there!"

The gilled-man protested. "I will not! Only Mermen like myself can enter!"

Dorak tightened his grip, leaving no room for negotiation. "I wasn't asking!"

At that moment, Kal, accompanied by a mage, intervened, helping to secure the merman in magical handcuffs that he couldn't break out of. "You are our prisoner until we get the artifact of the temple back and our friend. You will do as we say."

"And what if I refuse?" The merman challenged, defiance still flickering in his eyes.

Dorak, his patience worn thin, snarled back. "Then I will roast you for dinner, you fish-brained filet!"

Kal, reinforcing Dorak's threat, pressed a knife to the merman's throat. "Listen to the barbarian!"

Defeated and recognizing the gravity of his situation, the merman conceded. "Alright, I will help you get your friend back." He added, somewhat resigned. "By the way, the name is Merv."

Dorak, uninterested in pleasantries, released Merv's collar and forcefully guided him along. "No one asked you, fish breath."

The party, now with Merv in tow, returned to the palace to consult with Queen Alira. Upon seeing Merv, the queen expressed her curiosity. "I have never seen one of your kind. Why are you collaborating with the sorceress?"

Merv, resigned to his fate, admitted. "For power. She promises ultimate power when we help her take over the world."

The queen, outraged by the betrayal and the threat posed to her kingdom, declared. "You and your mistress have stolen an artifact of immense importance to us, and we need it back. Normally, I would imprison you and punish those who failed to protect it, but it seems we need your cooperation to retrieve the item. Assist us, or I will declare war on your entire race, leaving the seas barren of your people!"

Merv, irritated muttered. "Merlins are called Merlins, and we're from Merlienland! You surface dwellers never get this information right."

The queen, undeterred by his correction, reiterated her threat. "I don't care! Return our item, or prepare to become dinner!"

Kaley escorted Merv away as they prepared to depart. However, the queen requested Dorak and Kal to stay behind for a more private conversation. She expressed her disappointment. "Dorak, I welcomed you into my kingdom hoping you would aid us. Yet, a temple has been destroyed, and a priceless artifact is lost. What do you have to say for yourself?"

Dorak, filled with determination, proclaimed. "We did our best, and we will strive to improve. They took my friend as well. We've both suffered losses today, but I swear this will not happen again under my watch."

The queen, searching his eyes for sincerity, finally commanded, "retrieve our artifact by any means necessary."

As Dorak departed, Kal lingered. The queen turned to him. "You're an elf, and your loyalties are uncertain. Are you with us, or with your father? Keep an eye on that barbarian."

Kal, conflicted by the request, agreed. "Yes, Your Majesty," despite the turmoil it caused him.

That night, the weight of their failures and the daunting tasks ahead made rest elusive. Dorak, in particular, was tormented by the loss of his best friend and the disappointment he felt from the queen. The forces of evil seemed overwhelming, casting a shadow over their mission. As he lay awake, Dorak pondered the future, questioning if they were merely witnessing the beginning of a darker era. These thoughts haunted him into the early hours, as the dawn of their next challenge loomed.

Dorak at the Gate of Merlienland

Tarkas awoke in chains within a dimly lit cave, the cold dampness of the air clinging to his skin. He struggled against his restraints, the clinking of the chains echoing off the stone walls. "Good, you're awake," said a mage standing before him, shrouded in a dark hood, his short beard barely visible, and a scar slashing across his eye adding to his menacing appearance.

"Where am I?" Tarkas inquired, his voice echoing slightly in the cavernous space.

"You are in our lair. Mistress Zara is holding you here to learn more about you," the mage revealed, his tone devoid of warmth.

"Tell me who you are and why are you stealing magic?" Tarkas demanded, his frustration growing.

"I am Mage Plock, and we seek a new world order. Mistress Zara has been chosen to be our queen," Plock stated matter-of-factly. "Now, your turn. Who are you, and where did you get that bow?"

Tarkas hesitated, considering his response. "Will it get me out of these chains faster?"

"No, because your friends have our companion Merv, and you will serve as an excellent bargaining chip."

"I am Tarkas. I was a protector of the Crystal Caves. The bow was bestowed upon me by the gods to thwart your mistress's ambitions," Tarkas declared, defiance in his voice.

Plock rose to his feet, his interest seemingly satisfied. "That is all I needed to know." With that, he turned to leave the cave.

"You're just going to leave me here? Without food?" Tarkas called out after him.

Plock continued on, dismissing Tarkas's words as if they were whispers in the wind.

As the hours passed, Tarkas could sense that his captors were outside the cave but too far to hear his calls. The night enveloped the cave in coldness, and Tarkas wondered if anyone would come for him or if he was left to perish alone.

Unexpectedly, he was awakened from a restless sleep by the rattle of chains being unlocked. A hooded figure stood before him. "Plock, is that you?" Tarkas inquired, squinting in the dim light.

The figure paused, then removed his hood, revealing his identity. "No, recognize me now?" he asked.

The sight of familiar green eyes jolted Tarkas's memory. "Airis, you're alive. Why are you involved in all of this? What is going on?"

"Shhh." Airis flicked a spark of blue lighting at the locks, freeing them. "I will explain everything, but for now, I'm going to help you escape."

Once freed, Tarkas and Airis stealthily exited the cave, sneaking past the camp. Airis grabbed Tarkas's bow as they made their way to a clearing a safe distance from the camp. There, in a spontaneous act, Airis embraced Tarkas and kissed him.

Tarkas, taken aback, pushed Airis away. "What was that?"

"I have missed you," Airis confessed, his voice laced with emotion.

Tarkas, still reeling, demanded answers. "I've missed you too, but you need to explain yourself. What happened to you? I thought you died?"

Airis shared his story. "I didn't die. I used the boar attack years ago as my chance to escape. You know I always felt like an outsider for being the only magic user among the protectors. I had to find my path, and I did. I met Mistress Zara, a powerful sorceress who taught me so much. But I've missed you."

"Then why fake your death? And are you and the sorceress...?" Tarkas pondered aloud, seeking clarity.

Airis clarified. "I left without telling anyone because I had asked Gorak for permission to leave before, and he refused, citing our duty to protect the Crystal Caves. And no, Mistress Zara and I are not a couple; she's just been an incredible mentor."

"Funny how you always felt like the outsider when I was the adopted one." Tarkas gazed deeply into Airis's eyes, seeking answers to the turmoil within him. "So, the other night at the camp?"

"I let you go," Airis confessed softly, leaning in with the intent of a kiss.

Tarkas hesitated, his emotions conflicted. "Hold on, you seem to care about me and miss me, but do you realize I died during your attack on the caves? Everyone perished; me and Dorak were the only survivors." He paused, the weight of his next words heavy in his heart. "Actually, I died too. The gods brought me back to life. You were part of the cause."

Airis exhaled deeply, a mixture of regret and sadness in his eyes. "I didn't directly kill you, she did, but you're right; I am responsible for leading the attack to prove loyalty to her. I had no intention for everyone to be killed. We were blinded by our desire for the power within the caves."

Tarkas, filled with a swirl of emotions, questioned his fate. "Can I go now, or am I still your prisoner?"

Airis, his gaze intense and filled with complex emotions, replied. "I'm breaking the rules by helping you escape because I still care about you deeply. Unless you wish to join me? Yet, I yearn for us to spend one night together, reminiscent of the old times."

Memories of their younger days, filled with innocence and love, flooded Tarkas's mind. Despite the pressure of the situation, a part of him longed to return to those simpler times. Yielding to his heart's desire, he responded to Airis's affection. "I'm yours."

As Airis spread his cloak on the ground, they found solace in each other's arms, their passionate embrace a temporary escape from the world's chaos. For a brief moment, time seemed to stand still, transporting them back to their youthful days, untouched by the burdens they now bore.

Waking before dawn, Tarkas contemplated his next move, the quiet of the early morning amplifying his inner conflict. Grasping his bow and donning his armor, he wrestled with the thought of leaving Airis behind. The duty to his friends and the strategic advantage he represented weighed heavily against his longing for a few more stolen moments with Airis.

As he sat pondering, Airis awoke, surprised to see Tarkas still there. "Tarkas, why haven't you left? That was your chance to escape."

Tarkas, releasing a heavy sigh, confessed. "I know, but I'm needed as a bargaining chip. Yet, there's a part of me that yearns for just a few more nights with you."

Airis stood up, pulling Tarkas into an intense, passionate kiss, his hands tenderly caressing Tarkas's shoulders. Their reunion on the rock was abruptly interrupted by the cold, authoritative voice of the sorceress. "What is this?"

Airis quickly disengaged from the kiss, attempting to mask their true emotions. "Mistress, I was just having some fun with the prisoner."

"Don't lie to me; that was more passionate than just having fun," the sorceress countered, approaching them with a menacing grace. She extended her hand, adorned with long, claw-like nails, and gently traced Tarkas's face, her touch icy. "What is this man to you?"

Airis exhaled, caught in the revelation of their past. "He was my lover before I met you, and we were merely having a reunion."

The sorceress's gaze narrowed as she scrutinized Tarkas. "He is from the Crystal Caves and could provide us with valuable information about his companions."

"Yes," Tarkas managed to say, despite the looming threat.

Her nails dug slightly into his neck, her threat clear. "You will divulge what we wish to know, and you can have your reunion with Airis. If not, I have no qualms about ending your life. I don't need to return you alive to your friends. Understood?"

With the sorceress's grip tightening around his throat, Tarkas struggled for air but managed to nod in agreement.

"Yes, he will comply. I'll ensure it. I will be responsible for Tarkas until we arrange the trade," Airis interjected, his voice carrying a mix of desperation and determination.

"Tarkas, that's his name," she mused, locking eyes with him for a tense moment. "No attempts to escape, and you will follow orders. Then you may stay." Finally, she released her grip, allowing Tarkas to breathe freely again.

Gasping for air, Tarkas quickly agreed. "Yes, mistress, I understand."

The sorceress announced their imminent departure. "Alright, we are moving camp. I will send a message to your friends to inform them of the meeting point." With that, she turned and walked back towards the camp.

Tarkas was left with a sinking feeling in his stomach, realizing the gravity of the situation. The fleeting moments of passion with Airis had ensnared him in a precarious position, one that could jeopardize not only his safety but also that of his friends. As the sorceress's figure disappeared into the distance, Tarkas was left to ponder the cost of his devil's bargain, the weight of his choices hanging heavily in the balance.

Dorak and the others approached the mage's cabin nestled in the foothills of the woods. Dorak, puzzled by their detour, questioned, "Explain to me again why we have to stop at this mage's house?"

"It's because we lack magical abilities, and these mage brothers are powerful allies who can assist us. Plus, we're on a tight schedule; the sorceress won't be able to use the red stone without Merv," Kaley explained. After dismounting their gryphons, Dorak took a moment to retch, still uneasy from the flight.

Approaching the door, Kaley knocked assertively. "Kaste and Plock, it's Kaley. Open up; I need your assistance."

The door creaked open, revealing a stern face. "Plock is no longer with us. What do you want?"

Surprised by the response, Kaley stammered. "I'm so sorry; I had no idea Plock had passed."

"He didn't die; he's just dead to me," Kaste clarified, stepping back to allow them entry.

Kaley wedged her foot in the door to prevent it from closing. "Regardless, we still need your help," she insisted.

Kaste, resigned, let them into his home. They followed him as he moved through the house. "We're up against an evil sorceress wielding magic beyond our means," she explained.

Kaste settled into his chair, his interest piqued. "A sorceress? Wearing a necromancer's skull mask and clad in black leather armor?"

"Yes, that's her. Do you know her?" Kaley inquired.

"That's the witch who ensnared my brother. He became bewitched by her power, eventually forsaking our family's values. I had no choice but to disown him," Kaste recounted, his voice laced with bitterness.

"We share your disdain for her. She's responsible for the death of Dorak's people, the theft of the artifact from the Elven temple, and has now kidnapped our friend," Kaley explained, nodding towards Merv. "This is Merv; he's associated with her and is our captive for now."

Upon hearing this, Kaste's expression hardened. He struck Merv with a forceful blow. "Consider that a message for your mistress of evil!"

Merv, nursing his jaw, protested. "Ow! Why do you people keep hurting me? My mistress doesn't treat me this way."

Lira, checking Merv's injury, remarked. "Given the circumstances, you might want to brace yourself for more of this."

"So, you're planning a meetup with her?" Kaste deduced.

"Yes, she needs Merv to gain access to Merlienland. We're hoping to exchange him for Tarkas," Kaley stated.

Kaste pondered their situation briefly. Suddenly, a tapping at the window caught their attention. A black bird was pecking at the glass, a note clasped in its beak. Kaste approached, opened the window, and took the note, reading it aloud to the room, the content of which held the potential to change their course of action significantly.

Kaste carefully unfolded the note, his eyes scanning the message swiftly before reading it aloud for the group to hear: "We have your friend Tarkas, and you have our merman. We will meet you in 3 days at the gates of Merlienland for an exchange. Do you agree?"

Without a moment's delay, Dorak responded assertively to the bird. "We will be there!"

As the bird took flight and disappeared into the distance, Lira questioned, puzzled. "Did he just scare the bird away?"

Kaste, understanding the nature of the message carrier, clarified. "No, the bird was a familiar. It received the answer and has now returned to inform its master." He paused for a brief moment, then decisively added. "I will help train you. Let's go outside and start."

As they stepped outside, they were confronted with a gruesome scene. An Entelodon, commonly known as a Hell Pig, a monstrous and voracious creature, was devouring one of their gryphons while the other desperately attempted to escape. Enraged by the sight, Dorak's shout pierced the air, causing the beast to pause and lock eyes with him. The momentary standoff ended as the beast fled, leaving Dorak seething. "That was my steed, you bastard!" he exclaimed, before impulsively giving chase to the hell pig.

Kaste turned back to the bewildered group, inquiring. "Is this kind of behavior normal for him?"

"He has a lot of anger issues," Kal admitted, casting a glance towards the direction Dorak had run off.

Kaste, understanding the gravity of the situation but recognizing the urgency of their mission, asked. "Should we wait for him?"

"He possesses a magic sword; I don't think he's in as much need of the training as we are," Lira noted, her concern for Dorak mingled with the practicality of their predicament.

Acknowledging her point, Kaste concurred. "Alright, no time to waste. Let's get started."

Dorak sprinted through the forest, pursuing the hell pig that was easy to track due to the trail of blood it was leaving behind. He chased the creature for miles, patient for it to grow weary. Eventually, Dorak traced it back to its lair and watched from the bushes, biding his time until the beast would succumb to exhaustion. He observed as it settled down to rest, scrutinizing the flat, stony landscape for an advantageous position. Stealthily, he approached the foothill of the cave, careful not to disturb the resting beast. Climbing to the top of the cave, Dorak positioned himself directly above the sleeping creature and leaped onto its back, firmly grasping the tusks on the side of its face.

The beast erupted into a frenzy, kicking and struggling in an attempt to dislodge Dorak. Using all his might, Dorak wrestled with the creature, striving to maintain his grip. Despite a fierce struggle, Dorak was eventually thrown off. Yet, undeterred, he locked eyes with the beast, a mutual rage simmering between them. Dorak charged once more, and after a prolonged battle, the creature finally relented, both of them exhausted by the ordeal.

Dorak, embracing an unexpected truce, fell asleep in the cave with the hell pig's head resting in his arms. Upon waking, he found the beast had not harmed him; instead, it had procured food—a hare. Dorak prepared a fire, cooking the hare and sharing the meal with his newfound companion. As they ate, Dorak gazed into the beast's eyes, sensing a profound understanding between them. "I will call you Brimstone," he decided, and the Hell Pig snorted in what seemed like agreement.

With their bond cemented, Dorak mounted Brimstone, and they rode back to Kaste's house. Upon arrival, Brimstone's presence caused a stir, particularly with the gryphon, which reacted defensively. Dorak's command restored peace, showcasing his newfound leadership over these creatures.

"Wow, Dorak, you're back! We weren't sure what happened to you," Lira expressed her relief.

"I had to tame my new steed," Dorak replied, introducing Brimstone to the group.

"That's a hell pig! You expect to ride that? Those things aren't terrible!" Kal exclaimed in disbelief.

Dorak and Brimstone exchanged a knowing look. "We have an understanding. Besides, I didn't care much for flying anyway," Dorak stated, his bond with Brimstone evident to all.

The group, witnessing the unique connection between Dorak and the hell pig, nodded in acknowledgment.

"Alright, then, what's the plan, and when do we leave?" Dorak inquired, eager to proceed.

"We are leaving in the morning to confront the Sorceress at the agreed spot for the trade. This time, we're prepared to fight," Kal declared.

"And I'm coming with you. I want my brother back!" Kaste announced, determination in his voice.

Dorak smiled, rallying the group. "Good, then let's get ready!"

They spent the night training and finalizing their strategy. Merv, closely monitored, remained in the stables, with Lira occasionally bringing him food.

At dawn, they set off toward Merlienland, with Dorak riding Brimstone with Merv and Lira. Kal and Kaley flew on the gryphon, while Kaste kept pace on his horse. Arriving at the shore to Merlienland, they found the area deserted.

"Have we been set up?" Lira worriedly asked.

"No, we're just early," Merv reassured her, their eyes set on the horizon, ready for what was to come.

"Surely they won't keep us waiting much longer," Dorak stated, dismounting Brimstone. He assisted Lira and Merv off the beast, grounding themselves on the sandy shore. Surveying their surroundings, Dorak inquired. "Where is this place you call home?"

Merv gestured towards the vast expanse of water. "Beneath these waves lies my kingdom, a realm under the sea. I served as one of the king's advisors until he was assassinated. My ultimate aim is to secure power to safeguard my people and reclaim authority from the usurpers."

"And you believe allying with the Sorceress will help you achieve this?" Kaste questioned as he joined them.

Merv explained his position. "I'm indifferent to whose side I'm on, as long as my people are safe. If the sorceress promises to rule as a formidable power, I will accept her protection. And frankly, my people are better off without their magic; it only brings corruption."

"That's right, people don't need power. I need power," the Sorceress's voice rang out, cutting through the tension.

The group swiftly turned, confronting her arrival with her entourage, coinciding with Kal and another's landing. Dorak's gaze fixed on Tarkas, who appeared in shackles, his chains secured by Airis.

Seizing the moment, Dorak presented Merv. "Here's your fish friend. Now, give us Tarkas, and he's all yours!"

The Sorceress, unfazed, retorted. "Not so fast. Merv must retrieve the magic I desire."

Merv interjected. "I cannot fulfill that without the red stone."

"Very well, then. I will hand you the stone, and you shall descend," she conceded.

"Only after you've released Tarkas to us. You can command Merv as you wish once the exchange is complete," Dorak asserted firmly.

The Sorceress, with a sharp glare towards Dorak, ordered. "Fine, release the prisoner."

As Airis unlocked Tarkas's shackles, Tarkas leaned in, whispering, "You could come with us."

Airis whispered in return. "And you could stay."

With the chains released, Tarkas quickly joined Dorak's side. Dorak then pushed Merv towards the Sorceress, who handed over the red stone. "Go, retrieve the magic," she commanded.

Merv accepted the stone and plunged into the water, leaving those onshore in a tense standoff, awaiting his return. Dorak, though relieved to reunite with Tarkas, maintained a cautious demeanor, avoiding any conversation that might lower their guard.

It was Kaste who broke the silence, stepping forward with a request laced with years of estrangement and concern. "May I speak with my brother?" His voice carried a mix of hope and apprehension, seeking a moment of reconciliation amidst the unfolding drama.

"Only if your brother wants to talk to you," the sorceress said.

Plock looked at his brother and shook his head. "I have nothing to say."

Kaste snarled. "You bastard!"

Plock ignored his brother and stepped back.

Both sides stood at a stalemate while they waited for Merv or for the other side to make a move.

"You can go now; you got your friend. What more do you want?" the sorceress said.

"Well, I want my brother!" Kaste yelled.

"Well, he doesn't want you!" she yelled back. "So be gone."

"We want to wait till Merv returns," Kal said.

"What he does is none of your concern. Begone," she said.

"I don't think so; we are not going anywhere," Dorak shot back. He wanted to rip all of their heads off but knew it was best to wait until they made a move.

"Fine, then I will forcibly remove you," the sorceress declared, using her staff to shoot a bolt of magic at Dorak. Kal sprang forward, taking the blast on his shield, dispersing it into harmless sparks that fizzled out on the ground.

"This ends now," Kal roared, as Kaley and Lira, flanking him, rushed past him with their weapons drawn, They charged the sorceress together, who was forced to split her relentless barrage of lightning three ways. The distraction cost her dearly as the women leapt and dodged the scattered blasts while Dorak, swinging his Red Axe, spun waves of invisible force that absorbed the energy thrown at him. Tarkas's first arrow, whistled through the air at the sorceress; too fast to dodge, the arrow barely missed her as the wild air currents stirred by her lightning barrage pushed the shot a few inches wide. The sorceress, rallying her followers, commanded the elements, sending forth gusts of wind and arcs of lightning, attempting to disrupt the unity of Dorak and his allies. Airis, torn between his past and present, hesitated, his magic crackling ineffectively at his fingertips, the internal conflict evident in his stance.

Kaste, undeterred by his brother's rejection, focused his energy, stood well back of the whirling blades. In the chaos of battle he stood absolutely still, concentrating his energy as the others advanced.

Amidst the chaos, Merv emerged from the water, the red stone in hand, his return unnoticed in the heat of battle. His eyes quickly took in the scene, calculating where his allegiance would cause the least harm to his own future plans. With only a moment's hesitation, he passed the stone to the sorceress just as Dorak and Kal reached her.

With her power suddenly amplified by the stone, the sorceress called up the sea, and the sea answered. A towering wave rose behind her, boiling instantly into clouds of crackling steam as it tore through the stormcloud of arcane lightning surrounding her. It could not be parried or dodged as it roared toward Dorak and his companions, and came close enough to leave his face tingling and twitching before the electrified wave of steam broke and scattered only inches ahead of the group. Behind them, Kaste flinched as the red stone's crackling assault slammed against his magical barriers, but raised his voice to a shout as he held back the storm.

Merv, standing beside the sorceress, watched with a mixture of awe and fear as Kaste held back the assault. "Destroy them, Mistress," Merv pleaded. "You must stop them at any cost!"

"As you will," said the sorceress, raising the stone in one hand as she reached out for the terrified merman. She seized him with her free hand as it began to glow with a malevolent light and lifted him off the ground. The heroes watched in horror as she began to drain Merv's life force, his body growing frail and desiccated before their eyes.

Lira, driven by urgency and desperation, sprinted towards the sorceress, her sword raised for a strike. But she was halted abruptly by an invisible barrier that shimmered into view, protecting the sorceress from any physical attack.

Tarkas, observing Lira's thwarted attempt, quickly notched an arrow to his bow. With precise aim and a whisper of a prayer, he released the arrow, targeting the sorceress's hand. The arrow flew true, striking her and forcing her to release Merv, who fell to the ground, his body shockingly withered and drained.

The sorceress, momentarily distracted by the pain and surprise of the arrow's impact, faltered in her assault. Dorak, seizing the moment, charged forward with such sudden ferocity that even the crackling storm of lightning would not hold him back.

"Retreat! To me!" commanded the sorceress, signaling her group to withdraw. As they retreated, Kal unleashed an enchanted arrow, striking the Elf Mage in the back, ensuring he wouldn't escape unscathed.

Kaste felt the sudden weakening of the magical storm as the sorceress directed her energies elsewhere. "Stop her!" he cried. But he could not break his concentration until the storm was gone completely. As the companions closed in on them, the sorceress called up a shimmering pool of dark water from the ocean and leapt down through its surface into another place. Her minions followed her in the instant before the portal closed and an ordinary puddle of seawater splashed down over the vanished gateway.

Once the adversaries had vanished and their protective forcefield dissipated, Lira hurried to Merv's side. He was gasping for air, his strength waning. "My, ah, my power, she took it from me," he managed to articulate weakly.

"Do you want us to retrieve it for you?" Lira asked, concern evident in her voice.

"No, she betrayed me," Merv confessed with one of his diminishing breaths, the betrayal cutting deeper than any physical wound.

Kaste, in a desperate attempt to assist, scooped up some river water and gently splashed it on Merv, hoping to revive him before resorting to a healing spell. Unfortunately, it was clear that Merv was beyond the reach of any healing, his essence depleted.

"I'll avenge you, Merv," Lira promised, cradling him as his life ebbed away.

"Don't. I brought this upon myself. Thank you, Lira, for showing me kindness," Merv whispered, drawing his final breath.

A somber silence enveloped the group as they stood around Merv's body, processing the weight of his final moments. Kaste broke the silence, his voice tinged with determination. "If she's extracting powers from people only to kill them afterward, we must stop her before my brother suffers the same fate."

Kal, puzzled, questioned. "But how was she able to extract his magic? Typically, magic users can't assimilate different types of magic."

Tarkas contributed. "I believe she's developing a method to overcome those limitations. I overheard bits of it during my captivity but couldn't grasp the full extent."

The group realized the importance of Tarkas's insights. "What else did you witness or hear? We need all the information you can provide," Lira urged.

"I'll share everything en route to our next destination. But for now, what should we do with Merv's body?" Tarkas inquired, the gravity of the situation weighing heavily on them.

Gazing at Merv's desiccated remains, Dorak suggested. "Let's return him to the water; it's where he belongs."

With a collective nod, they solemnly carried his body to the water's edge, allowing him to sink back into the depths from which he came. They shared a moment of silence, honouring his memory.

Then, turning their attention to the task ahead, Dorak asked, "Where to next?"

Kal turned to Kaste, recalling the earlier encounter. "I hit the Elf Mage with one of those enchanted arrows you mentioned could be traced."

"Good, and yes, I can trace it. We need to track them down and intercept them before any harm comes to my brother," Kaste affirmed, his resolve firm.

"They mentioned something about the Swamps of Molav, but I'm unsure of the exact location," Tarkas added, his memory straining.

"That's too far off; it can't be their immediate goal," Kaste reasoned. "They're planning something significant. Let's head in their direction, and once we make camp, we'll compile what we know."

Dorak and the Mage's College

The party set up camp and gathered around the fire to regroup. Kaley had sustained a gash on her arm, and Kaste was attentively tending to her wound. Amidst the quiet, Kal, eyeing Tarkas with suspicion, broke the silence. "So, what did they do to you in those three days, Tarkas?"

"Torture, and barely fed me. They interrogated me constantly, asking numerous questions. I only told them who we were and that we were coming for them," Tarkas replied, his voice tinged with fatigue.

As Kaste finished bandaging Kaley, he turned his attention to Tarkas. "They beat you; please show me your injuries, and I will heal you."

Tarkas hesitated, uncomfortable with revealing his wounds, but eventually, he relented and showed his back, which was covered in a mix of old, necrotic wounds and fresh whip marks, scratches, and bites. He felt a knot of apprehension in his stomach, hoping Kaste wouldn't probe too deeply.

"Did they inflict necrotic damage on you?" Kaste inquired, examining the marks closely.

Tarkas shook his head, his expression solemn. "No, I died over a month ago. The flesh of the dead does not keep so well as the flesh of the living. The lash marks, though, are recent."

Kaste applied a healing cream to the necrotic areas and channeled his magic to mend the flesh as best he could. After a few moments, he expressed his concern. "I did my best, but some of these will take more time to heal. I'm worried about how much of your body is compromised."

"I understand," Tarkas responded. "We don't know if I'm on borrowed time or if these wounds will just take longer to heal since I was dead for a week before being revived."

"I will consult more of my books on this subject and keep an eye on these wounds to ensure they aren't worsening," Kaste assured him.

"Thank you for that," Tarkas said, grateful for Kaste's expertise and care.

Kal, still seeking answers, pressed further. "So, what exactly did you tell them about us?"

"I only spoke of myself and Dorak, relating to the Crystal Caves. When they asked about you, Kal, and Lira, I simply said you were following us—I didn't disclose who you really are. And I know Dorak wouldn't mind me mentioning our origins," Tarkas explained.

"Of course not," Dorak interjected fiercely. "I will crush them and make them regret ever attacking the Crystal Caves."

"There's more," Tarkas continued, sensing the gravity of his next revelation. "I can tell you who the wizard is, and you're not going to like it." Dorak's eyes narrowed intensely on Tarkas, bracing for the answer.

Tarkas paused, taking a deep breath to steady himself. "It's Airis," he revealed.

Dorak's response was visceral, a roar of fury echoing through the camp. "ARGH!! THAT ASSHOLE! I WILL MURDER HIM!!"

Lira, feeling confused and out of the loop, inquired. "Who is Airis?" As Dorak erupted in anger, kicking stones in his frustration,

Tarkas explained calmly. "He grew up with us and was also a member of the Protectors of the Crystal Caves. We thought he died a few years ago, but it turns out he left to pursue deeper knowledge in magic."

Dorak, unable to contain his fury, stormed back into the conversation. "NEXT TIME I SEE HIM, I WILL RIP OUT HIS THROAT! ARRGH!!"

Lira, taken aback by Dorak's intense reaction, asked. "Are you not upset by this?"

Tarkas replied. "I am very upset, but unlike Dorak, I don't have rage issues, and I've had three days to process this information. It's tragic, really."

Kal, looking to understand more, asked. "What else can you tell us about your time there?"

"They have a base in the mountains near a place called Alwyndia and plan to head there soon. That's all I know, except that she is amassing power," Tarkas disclosed.

"Alwyndia City, that's not far from here. That's good because we're heading there," Kaste interjected, seeing a strategic advantage.

Dorak, still simmering with anger, challenged him. "Who said we were going anywhere? Since when do you make the plans!"

Kaste, unfazed by Dorak's outburst, responded calmly. "Calm down, you barbarian. I need to consult books on how to heal your friend. As we've seen, we don't yet have the power to defeat her, and if her power is growing, we need more than what we have here. Brute force and enchanted weapons aren't going to cut it. In the mage school they have a school of the mystic arts there, where I can learn more about healing Tarkas."

Dorak grudgingly acquiesced. "Fine, do what you need. I just want her and Airis dead!"

"And they will be, once we have the power to defeat them," Kaste assured him.

Tarkas, trying to bring some order, suggested. "I think we need to rest for the night, and then we can head to the city tomorrow. Do you know the way? I've never been nor heard of this place."

Kaste nodded. "I went to school there. I can guide us. And yes, sleep sounds like a good idea."

After a night's rest, the group set off early in the morning for Alwyndia City. The journey took about a day, and as they approached the outskirts, Dorak and Tarkas were taken aback by the sheer size of the city and the unfamiliar machines lined along its fortress walls. Lira, curious about the city's defenses, asked. "What are those metal things on top of the wall?"

"Those are cannons. They shoot balls at the enemies," Kaste explained, noting the group's amazement at the city. "Have none of you ever been to the city before or seen cannons?"

Tarkas responded. "No, Dorak and I are from a small rural community. The city near us was never this big or advanced."

"Same here. I might be from a walled city, but nothing this large," Kal added.

Kaste nodded, understanding their awe. "I see. Well, there's going to be a bit of an adjustment then. I'm familiar with this place because I attended the school of magic here; it's like a second home to me." He led them through the gates of the city.

Dorak, puzzled by the conversation, inquired. "You've used this word 'school' before—what is that?"

Kaste, slightly surprised by the question, explained. "A school is a building where people go to learn skills to help them in the future; in this case, magic. It's taught by teachers."

"I know what a teacher is, but I didn't know you had buildings for this. Where I'm from, you learn from the leader and your mother," Dorak commented.

Kal shrugged. "Don't look at me—I didn't go to a school. I had a private tutor, so he's not that far off."

Kaste, slightly dismayed by their responses, asked. "Has no one here actually gone to a formal school?"

They all shook their heads. Kaley spoke up. "As someone who has traveled almost as much as you have, Kaste, I will tell you that this city and school are unique. I'm not as shocked by this tech because I've heard of this city, but it's not something you'll see elsewhere in the region."

Kaste replied. "Well then, you will all have fun exploring the city."

As they entered through the city gates, they were stopped by the guards. "Halt, what brings you to Alwyndia City?"

Kaste presented his mage certificate. "I'm associated with the Mage School, and these are my companions."

The guards scrutinized the document before nodding. "You may proceed."

They ventured into the city, passing brightly colored stone buildings and others made of wood. As they walked past the marketplace, Kaste pointed towards a large tower in the distance to the right. "That is the mage's school."

Lira, curious about their next steps, asked. "Are we going there now?"

"I was thinking that we could settle into town first, grab a room at the inn, and get some food. I feel we are going to be here for a few days," Kaste suggested.

Tarkas, slightly annoyed, responded. "I thought we were going to get straight to work since it's still daylight? Do we need to talk to the monarchs here about the impending threat?"

"I don't think we have to worry about an attack here. Yes, we need to talk to the mages, but I thought we could do that in the morning," Kaste replied.

Dorak glared at him, suspicion in his eyes. "You're stalling. What is going on?"

Kaste, feeling defensive, admitted. "I get nervous before going back there. I would like to let off some steam before we go."

Dorak snarled, but before he could say anything more, Kal interjected. "That's fine. Just get us in there so we can discuss everything. We don't know how much time we have before their next move, and you need to treat Tarkas."

Kaste sighed, resigned to the urgency. "I guess we will go today."

They walked through the city, noting it was much farther than they had expected. "How big is this place? I'm from Centoria and thought we had a big city, but this is huge. And the city walls—it's a lot of stone," Kal remarked.

"When we get to the mage's school, you'll see it's on a cliffside of a mountain, just above the walls. The rumors are that this city was carved out of a former mountain, and the mage's school is the oldest structure of the city, built into part of the original mountain. There is evidence of this in the structure of the buildings, but it's hard to believe anyone could have done it. That's also why the buildings are different colors—they are naturally colored from the stone they were carved from," Kaste explained.

They continued their long walk until they started up the stone-carved stairs of the mountain. As the sun began to set, they looked back on the city and saw the city walls, realizing the truth in what Kaste had said about the city being carved from a single stone. They paused to rest and take in the view.

"Why didn't we just fly the gryphon up here and save time?" Lira asked.

"There's nowhere for it to stay here, and there's a magic barrier keeping unwanted guests out," Kaste explained.

"Will we be wanted?" Captain Kaley asked.

"I don't see why not," Kaste replied, continuing the walk to the school.

They eventually reached the entrance of the mage's school, an imposing structure partially embedded in the mountain. Kaste led the way, his nervousness palpable, but he remained determined to help his friends and confront his past. The grandeur of the school, with its ancient architecture and mystical aura, made it clear they were entering a place of immense power and knowledge. The group, despite their exhaustion, felt a renewed sense of purpose as they prepared to seek the aid of the mages within.

They arrived at the gates of the mage's school where a projection of one of the mages appeared, beginning to speak. Before the message could progress, Kaste waved his hands, murmured some words, and a flash of light created a glowing arch. He stepped through briskly. "Come on, before the door closes," he urged.

"What was that?" Tarkas asked, intrigued by the display of magic.

"It's a spell to bypass the lock. You need to know it to open the gate. I'm just tired of the message that plays; I've heard it too many times in my youth," Kaste explained as they walked down the courtyard path towards the school. Soon, the mage they had seen in the projection materialized in front of them in the flesh. He was an older man with a long white beard, dressed in blue-greyish robes. "Kaste, you know you're supposed to listen to that message. It disrupts my magic when you cut the projection short. And who are your friends?"

"Master Dormir, it's always a pleasure to see you. Since you read minds, why don't you tell me who they are?" Kaste replied with a hint of snark.

"I can't read minds; I read energy patterns. But with you, it was always easy to guess what you were up to," Dormir corrected him with a slight chuckle. "So, what brings you here today? It's quite a surprise to see you."

"Well, as much as you thought I was a troublemaker back in the day, it's my brother this time. Plock has joined forces with a sorceress and a few others, and they are draining the planet of its magical powers. These are my new companions who have been affected by this," Kaste explained, indicating his group.

Dormir studied the group, then approached Tarkas with a curious gaze. "What are you?" he asked directly.

Tarkas, taken aback, replied. "What do you mean? I'm human, one of the last protectors of the Crystal Caves."

"No, that's not it. There is something old and strange about you. I haven't felt a presence like this in a long time. Tell me more," Dormir insisted, extending his hand to hover near Tarkas, sensing the unusual energies around him.

"I was dead for a week and the waters of the Fountain of life brought me back to life. I'm still recovering from that. Is that what you sense?" Tarkas frowned.

"That's close enough to give me a clue," Dormir replied, turning around. "Follow me, and we will figure out what is going on."

They all followed the master into the stone tower and entered a grand hall where the walls were lined with shelves filled with bottles and plants. They continued past this to what looked like Dormir's office. He sat down in his large, ornately carved wooden chair. "Now, tell me the situation and why you are here."

Dorak began to recount the tale of their journey and the challenges they had faced, and Kaste continued the story, focusing on the recent developments. Dormir listened intently and then said. "Alright, Kaste, you may use the resources and stay in the city for as long as you need. I will have word sent to the Monarch about this. There are rooms in the tower where you can all stay. Kaste, you can go to the library and do your research, and Tarkas, I would like to speak with you further. The rest of you, get settled in; there will be dinner in an hour."

As the night wore on and they prepared for bed, Kaste approached the group. "Hey, I was going to head into town for some late-night fun. I was wondering if any of you would like to join me?"

"It's dark; will we be able to see our way?" Lira asked.

Kaste snapped his fingers, and a ball of light appeared. "With this, you will." He snapped them again, and the light turned off. "So, who's with me?"

"What kind of late-night fun?" Kal inquired.

"Well, there's the bar that's open all night, and there's my favorite place, the brothel if you want to join?" Kaste offered.

Kal and Tarkas nodded. "Yeah, we'll join you."

Lira spoke up. "This sounds interesting. Does the brothel have variety?"

"They have something for everyone," Kaste winked.

"Then I'll tag along," Lira decided.

"Alright, Dorak, Kaley, are you two coming?" Kaste asked.

"I prefer to rest, thank you," Kaley responded.

"How can anyone think of anything besides the goal at hand? I too will rest," Dorak stated.

Tarkas laughed. "Typical Dorak. Yeah, it looks like it's just us four; let's get going."

They snuck out of the tower quietly and made their way to the city. When they arrived at the brothel, the madam at the front smiled at Kaste. "Kaste, you're back in town and you brought friends! It's always nice to see you."

Kaste grinned. "You know I wouldn't miss the chance to come visit. Is Jade working?"

"She sure is. I'll tell her to meet you in the room," the madam responded.

"You can ask her for anything; they have it all," Kaste smirked and walked through the silk curtain.

The madam turned to the group, a welcoming smile on her face. "So, what will you be having?"

Kal spoke up first. "Do you have a female elf?"

"We sure do," she responded cheerfully.

"Any charming guy will do for me," Lira added.

"Can do. And you?" the madam asked, turning to Tarkas.

"I'll take a charming guy as well," he replied with a smile.

She beamed at them. "All of you, come with me. I have just the people for you." They all followed her behind the curtain to the back, where they encountered a vast room adorned with silk cushions and beauties of all races and genders lounging gracefully. This was a new and extravagant experience for them. The brothel in Centoria City was nowhere near as luxurious as this one and didn't offer nearly the same variety of companions.

It was late into the night, and Kal turned to his companion, Kleo. "It was so nice being with you. Are there many elves outside of Kelonia city?"

She embraced him on the bed. "Not many. My parents left during the war and ended up here. I joined the brothel because it pays well. Being one of the only elves in the city makes me more marketable. And I enjoy being here."

"I enjoyed being with you too. I grew up being the only elf in my city and left to learn about my culture and give my life meaning, but I haven't seen too many elves yet because I couldn't stay in the city too long. But now, I have my cousin with me who is teaching me things," Kal shared, a note of longing in his voice.

"Not to sound like I'm soliciting you for more money, but if you're in town for a bit, we could totally meet up again and talk about elf culture if you wanted," Kleo suggested softly.

He held her close. "That would be wonderful."

The morning light filtered through the curtains, and Tarkas awoke lying in a pile of pillows on a padded mat. He blinked his eyes open to see Kaste standing above him, an expression of concern mixed with curiosity on his face.

"Did you sleep well?" Kaste inquired.

"Oh no, I slept all night. Am I in trouble for staying here longer?" Tarkas asked, reaching for his clothes.

"No, it's fine. I think we were all tired and just slept here. Did you enjoy yourself?" Kaste sat down on some pillows next to Tarkas.

"Yeah, it was fun, but wow, these pillows are amazing. I don't think I've ever slept on a bed this soft. It was nice. I'm used to the ground," Tarkas said, sitting up.

"Well, you can get used to it while we're in the city," Kaste remarked, giving Tarkas a once-over. "Hey, I wanted to ask you a couple of questions."

"Sure, ask away," Tarkas responded.

"When I was treating your wounds, I noticed that there were more than just whip marks and necrotic flesh, but also some bites and scratches. Care to explain that?" Kaste inquired.

Tarkas paused for a moment to think about how he was going to explain this. "Airis and I were lovers back when we were younger. Myself, Dorak, and Airis all grew up together. Airis and I were close, but he faked his death to go learn magic when Dorak's father, Gorak, refused to let him break his oath. Me and Dorak had no idea about this until I was kidnapped. And well, the bite marks you saw well, Airis and I we rekindled our relationship. It was nice to be with him for a few moments because I knew, and he knew too, that once I left, we would be enemies and that he would be subject to the punishment of the laws of the Crystal Caves. So, when we catch them, you will have to stand back and let Dorak decide his punishment, since Dorak is the new leader," Tarkas explained.

"I see. So, who died and made Dorak the leader?" Kaste asked.

"Tribal law. The child of the leader gets first claim to be the new leader when their parent dies, and then if anyone wants to challenge for the role, they can. But there are only three of us left, one is a traitor and therefore disqualified, and then there's me, but I was adopted, and normally that would complicate things, but there is no point. I must prepare for the day that when we defeat Airis and Zara that the order of the Crystal Caves is over, and all outstanding vendettas are cleared," Tarkas elaborated.

"Wow, that is heavy. Thank you for explaining that. And I can see why you would not talk about this openly. I assume you don't know the other members of the group that well," Kaste said, continuing to scrutinize Tarkas's body. "Since we're both here and I know you're interested in men, I was wondering if you would be interested in having some fun with me?"

Tarkas raised an eyebrow, a half-smile forming on his lips. "Was this your plan all along? You could have just asked."

Kaste leaned in closer, his gaze intense. "I just wanted to be sure. There's something about you that draws me in."

"If it's acceptable here, then I see no reason to decline. You've caught me at a vulnerable moment," Tarkas joked lightly.

They shared a passionate kiss, their embrace lingering under the subtle glow of the daylight.

"Get out of the garden, you dumb barbarian! We need to tend that for our food!" a short mage shouted at Dorak, who had been found sleeping among the greenery.

Dorak rose, frowning at the diminutive accuser. "Who are you calling dumb? If your beds were more comfortable, I wouldn't need to sleep in the only patch of grass on this mountain!" he retorted.

"There is nothing wrong with our beds, you oaf!" the mage shot back.

Dorak stared him down. "I didn't sleep on any of your plants; your garden is fine!"

Kal hurried over upon hearing the commotion. "Dorak, calm down. We'll talk to them about getting you a better bed. Don't rip this mage in half—he's already short as it is."

Both Dorak and the mage glared at Kal. Realizing his mistake, Kal called out, "Where's Tarkas? He's needed here."

"Him and Kaste stayed behind; I haven't seen them yet. I'll go get the headmaster," Lira replied and soon returned with Master Dormir.

"Stop fighting, both of you. The garden is fine; no harm came to it," Master Dormir addressed them, then turned to Dorak. "What's the problem with our beds? They're made from the finest straw we can get."

"They're too soft, and it's too quiet inside. I prefer the ground," Dorak grumbled.

Master Dormir sighed. "I'm sorry to hear that, Dorak. We'll find a suitable sleeping arrangement for you. Until then, no more fighting. Let's get on with the day. Has anyone seen Tarkas and Kaste?"

"They stayed behind at the brothel. I don't know when they'll be back," Lira informed.

Master Dormir sighed again, clearly frustrated. "Alright, I'll handle this." He stormed off towards his office.

Around lunchtime, Kaste and Tarkas returned. Dorak was at the table, devouring several bowls of food when he spotted them. "Hey, Tarkas, you're back. The master is looking for you. Also, if you're hungry, ask the chef for some food. We weren't sure when you'd return, so I ate yours. Just a warning, they don't provide enough food here."

Tarkas laughed, while Kaste had an annoyed look on his face. "Alright, I will go get some food. It's good to see you're eating well. Kaste and I had breakfast before we came back, but we could definitely enjoy some lunch."

They returned a few moments later with bowls of food. "You're right, they don't give much food," Tarkas observed, eyeing his modest serving of grains and meat. He then placed some red stalks on the table. "I did manage to get you some rhubarb for after; I know how much you love it."

Dorak grabbed one of the stalks and took a big bite. "Thanks," he mumbled appreciatively.

As they ate, Master Dormir entered the hall. "Tarkas, you're here—good, I need to speak with you."

Kaste looked up from his meal. "What about me?"

"No, you're not needed at the moment; you can go do your research," Dormir said, then gestured to Tarkas. "Come, follow me."

When they reached Dormir's office, Tarkas sat down in the chair across from him. "Why did you want to see me?"

"Tarkas, what do you know about your parents?" Dormir inquired.

"Nothing, I was a foundling. Gorak, the chief, took me in and raised me. I drank from the Crystal Caves as a baby and was given the gift of high intelligence. I was trained to be an archer, and Dorak is like a brother to me. That's all. Why does this matter?" Tarkas asked, puzzled.

"Because there is something different about you. I have been trying to read your energy patterns, and they are something much older. It's not like your friend Dorak; your ability comes from somewhere else."

"Well, I was dead for a week, and the waters of the Fountain of Life brought me back. Is that what you're sensing?" Tarkas inquired.

Dormir shook his head. "No, it's not that. I will tell you a secret: the Fountain of Life's water is the same that flows through the Crystal Caves. The only difference is that the crystals filter the water, making it safe to drink. The gods probably approved you to drink the water directly from the source because of your unique heritage. There's more to your story, Tarkas. We need to delve deeper into your past to uncover the truth. Have you ever tried spellcasting?"

Tarkas shook his head. "No, my friend Airis was the only spellcaster, and he eventually betrayed us. But as kids, we would play, and he would practice magic while I tried to copy it; it didn't work." Tarkas smiled, reminiscing about the good times he had as a child with Airis.

Dormir observed Tarkas's demeanor for a moment. "I have a theory, and it will require another expert to come in, someone much older than me. She will know."

"Do I have to travel again? Because, one, I kind of like it here, and two, we came here for your help to fight Airis and Zara," Tarkas lamented.

"Oh no, not at all. You are staying here, and so are your friends. You will have the most protection, and we are not far from their base. No, this person I will call for, and he will come to us."

"Great, is that all? Can I go now?" Tarkas asked.

"One more thing," Dormir continued. "your friend Dorak had some issues this morning; he was found sleeping in the garden, complaining our beds were too soft for him, and he eats so much. What do we do? I don't like his temper."

Tarkas laughed. "Call me next time; I can handle him. He loves sleeping outside; he never liked tents and always preferred to be on watch duty. And you've seen his size; he's going to eat a lot. But he will work for it if you put him to work. He will also hunt his own food if you let him."

"I see," Dormir sighed. "It has been a long time since I've dealt with barbarians. I'm going to have to get used to it."

Tarkas chuckled. "I'll keep him in line; don't you worry. He's like a brother to me. But am I free to go now?"

"Yes, but I recommend that you don't leave the school. You and your friends are protected here, and until we know more, I would like to keep you somewhere safe. At dinner, I will talk to you and your friends about our plan going forward."

"Sir, I thank you for your efforts, but over the last while, I have seen these people break down all magic and destroy all in their path. What makes you think that they will be stopped here?"

"Oh no, you have it all wrong. They may still be able to put up a good fight, but here your essence is blocked, and they will not be able to detect you. Please stay here so we can keep you safe. I feel they may have a larger interest in you," Dormir yawned. "Now, if there are no further questions, you may go."

Tarkas left the office, pondering what had been said, and began to question his past and who he really was. There was not much else to do but wait for dinner and find out what the plan was.

At dinner, when they had all gathered, Master Dormir approached their table and spoke. "I've given it some thought and consulted with my colleagues. Since you will all be here for a bit, I will assign tasks to keep you engaged while we plan for the next attack. Everyone will undergo magic defense training while here. Kaste, you can choose to study or join the training sessions. Dorak, I've arranged for you to stay and sleep near the garden in exchange for helping Master Verruca with the vegetable harvest. In return, you'll be allowed to eat as much as you need."

Dorak grunted in agreement, his expression showing a mix of resignation and satisfaction at the arrangement.

Dormir then turned his attention to Tarkas. "I have sent word to Grand Master Stellira and she will be here as soon as she can. So, for now, I suggest you all lay low and enjoy the school."

Kal, finishing his bite of food, raised a concern. "What about the king? Shouldn't we notify the monarch that we are here and inform them about the threat?"

Master Dormir paused, considering Kal's question. "We will address that, and that can be the plan for tomorrow. Until then, I want you all to rest and eat up; you have a busy day ahead."

They all resumed eating, understanding that this might be the last tranquil night they would have for some time as the situation was poised to escalate further.

Tarkas and the Archery Contest

"Can I leave, please?" Tarkas pleaded with Master Dormir. "I've been cooped up in this place for almost a week, and I want to see the city."

"Not until after Grandmaster Stellira has arrived," Dormir replied. "They will tell us what we need to know about you. Until then, we need you to stay here where they cannot detect you. I feel that Mistress Zara will want to get her hands on you."

Tarkas was doubtful. He had been close to Zara, and she had shown no interest in him. However, he knew that Airis would probably be interested in their location, and if they could sense him, it was better to stay hidden. Still, he just wanted to explore the city. He had never seen a city this advanced, with so many things to discover. His companions were allowed to leave at times.

After training for the day, he lay in his bed, restless, wondering how much longer this confinement would last. Dorak walked by.

"I have no idea how you can put up with those beds," Dorak commented.

Tarkas laughed. "I like comfy things, and this feels better on my back than the ground. But there's not much else to do here. I want to go out and explore."

"Then go! What are you afraid of? We're fearless!" Dorak said.

"It's not fear. It's out of respect for Master Dormir. I do want to talk to this Grandmaster when they arrive. And why hasn't the monarch come yet? We've been here almost a week," Tarkas replied.

"Well, if you're going to be listening to authority, I outrank all of them, and I tell you to do whatever you want. And if Airis and Zara show up, I'll gladly welcome a fight with them. I don't need this training; I just need to get close to them," Dorak declared.

"I'll think about it, but thanks for reminding me about home. I miss it, and I think I'm starting to forget it," Tarkas admitted.

"I know," Dorak said before walking away.

Tarkas lay on his bed, watching the sun go down. He had never been so bored in his life, and he was starting to feel aimless. He heard the dinner bell ring but didn't feel like getting up to eat. A while later, Kaste came to check on him.

"Hey, we didn't see you at dinner. What's going on?" Kaste asked.

"I wasn't hungry," Tarkas mumbled, rolling over on the bed.

"I would have brought you some leftovers, but Dorak ate them all," Kaste said, pausing for a moment. "Dorak mentioned that you're feeling a bit trapped here?"

Tarkas sighed. "Yeah. It's so boring here. I don't know what to do with myself, and I want to explore this city, even if we don't know how long we're going to be here."

"Well, why didn't you say so? I'll help you get out of here. I was a troublemaker when I was a student here—Master Dormir is so boring," Kaste said, sitting down on the stone bed.

Tarkas sat up. "But the enemy will detect us if I leave."

Kaste leaned in and kissed Tarkas. "Don't worry about them. I'm sure you're not on their priority list. But since we've been here, I've felt a surge in my magic like no other. So, I think with my magic and your bow, we could take them."

"I can take my bow through the city?" Tarkas asked.

"Yeah, lots of travelers come through here. They aren't worried. So, do you want to get out of here and have some fun?" Kaste winked.

"I do, but I'd like to find the monarch and tell them about what's going on," Tarkas said.

"Yeah, that's a good point. We sent a message to her the other day, but she hasn't replied. I wonder what's going on," Kaste pondered.

"Well then, let's go pay her a visit," Tarkas said, starting to get up.

"One moment." Kaste grabbed Tarkas's arm, stopping him. "It's late. We can't just go barging into the palace tonight."

"Then let's get a hotel and go in the morning. I want to do something now." Tarkas stood up, collecting his things.

Kaste stood up with him and kissed him again. "Yeah, let's go out and have some fun. I know a place." He went to his room and returned with his backpack. "Got all your stuff? Are you ready?"

"Yup. Now, how do we get out of here?" Tarkas followed Kaste through the basement of the school. They passed some things that looked like summoning circles and a storage room. "Are you sure this is the right way? It feels really creepy in here," Tarkas said.

"Yeah, this is exactly where people wouldn't want to go to get out. I found it when I was younger. This path takes you right down the mountain to the old delivery route. It also gets you past the shield spell that surrounds this entire place," Kaste explained.

As they reached the bottom of the stairs, Kaste put his arm across Tarkas's chest. "Shh, I hear something."

They stood against the wall, trying to listen to the conversation.

"Is Tarkas here?" a woman's voice said.

"He is. Do you want him now?" the man's voice asked.

"Not tonight. I'll come back for him. I just wanted to make sure he's here," she said.

"You say the word, and he'll be yours," he replied.

Kaste leaned in a bit closer to get a view of the people who were talking. His foot hit a rock on the steps, causing it to bounce down the stairs.

"What was that? Is someone there?" she called out.

"Rats, I'm sure. That sound was just the rats running around. No one knows about this path," the man said.

"Fine, but I'll be back. You know how to reach me," she said and left.

Kaste signaled to Tarkas to follow him. They rushed back up the stairs and hid behind a crate in the previous room until the other mage left. Once the coast was clear, they made their way out the door. When they were a distance away from the college, Tarkas stopped Kaste.

"Who was that talking?" Tarkas asked.

"Zara and a younger mage. I forget his name—he's new. But I don't know what she wants with you," Kaste replied.

"I don't know either. She let me go before, and Airis and I are over, so I have no business with her. But this makes me not want to go back to the college," Tarkas said.

Kaste nodded. "I'll cover for you if you want to stay in town. But right now, we should get you booked into the inn and plan our visit to the monarch tomorrow."

They made their way through the city and arrived at the inn. There was a restaurant bar downstairs and the inn upstairs. Tarkas stopped Kaste.

"Wait, how are we paying for this? I have no money because my tribe didn't use it. I appreciate you paying for the other night, but..."

"I have plenty of money, don't worry about it," Kaste said. He went up to the bar and asked Tarkas. "Do you need any food?"

"Yeah, that would be nice," Tarkas replied.

"Take a seat," Kaste said, and Tarkas sat down while Kaste spoke to the barkeep to rent a room and get a meal for Tarkas. A few moments later, Kaste returned to the table. "They'll bring the food in a moment, and we got the room upstairs."

"Thank you so much," Tarkas said, feeling unsettled. He looked at Kaste. "Why do you think Zara wants me? She had me, and she could have kept me."

"I think whatever Master Dormir sees in you, she's picked up on. She didn't realize it at the time, but now she wants you," Kaste said.

The food arrived shortly after. The cook placed a tray of meat stew on the table and commented. "That's a neat bow you've got there."

Tarkas, unsure how to respond, said. "Uh, thank you."

"I've never seen a bow like that. Where did you get it?" the cook asked.

Not wanting to reveal its origins, Tarkas replied. "I'm a protector of the Crystal Caves. It's my tribal bow. I've had it as long as I can remember."

"Crystal Caves? You're a barbarian archer?"

"In a few words, yes. But what is this about?" Tarkas asked.

"Well, there's an archery tournament coming up, and I thought maybe you were a part of it. But I've never seen someone from your tribe in town, and you're hanging out with a mage?" the cook said.

Tarkas thought about his next words carefully. "I'm definitely in town for the archery contest. And I know Kaste—"

"—We met because I've been studying the caves to understand how they get their magic. That's all," Kaste interrupted.

"I see, interesting. Well, enjoy your stay, guys," the cook said before leaving.

Kaste waited for the cook to leave, then whispered to Tarkas. "Do you want to sign up for the archery contest?"

"Well, what else was I supposed to say?" Tarkas replied.

"I guess you had no choice," Kaste admitted.

"I'm a darn good archer, so why can't I enter the contest?" Tarkas said as he ate his food.

"Alright, I'm not going to stop you. We can look into it in the morning," Kaste said.

It didn't take long for Tarkas to finish his food. They then made their way to the room. When Tarkas opened the door, he saw one bed in the medium-sized, basic room. Grinning at Kaste, he said. "One bed. Does that mean what I think it does?"

"Well, the rooms only have one bed each, but I wouldn't be disappointed," Kaste winked.

Tarkas kissed him, closed the door, and whispered in Kaste's ear. "Thank you."

In the morning, they ate their breakfast and made their way to the festival grounds for the archery contest to find out what was involved. Tarkas walked to the registration table. At the desk, there were two men—one wearing a tunic and the other in archer's leather gear. The man in the tunic looked at Tarkas and asked. "Name and where are you from?"

"Tarkas, of the Crystal Caves of Centoria."

The man in the archer gear stared at Tarkas. "Crystal Caves? We haven't had someone from there in years. You also look a little large to be an archer."

Tarkas grinned. "Well then, you'll be impressed by my skills."

The man in the tunic wrote something down. "Alright, the competition will start in the next hour. Just go over to the left and wait with the others. You, mage, need to stay with the spectators on the right."

Tarkas joined the group of archers, noticing that he was much larger than the others, who were tall and slim. He began to prepare his bow.

One of the men approached him. "Never seen you here before. Are you any good?"

Tarkas strung his bow. "Best in my village. What about you?"

"Last year's champion. Name's Skolsav, from the northern village of Skolagg. What about you?" Skolsav asked.

"I'm Tarkas, from the Crystal Caves of Centoria. I've never heard of your city, but this is the furthest I've been from home."

"I've never heard of yours either, but it's nice to have you here. I know I can beat all these other guys, so it'll be nice to see what you've got." He laughed and patted Tarkas on the back. "I want to know, though—why are you so large? Usually, archers are small and nimble."

"I keep getting that question, but I'll tell you: I'm one of the smallest in my village. My best friend Dorak is much bigger than me. But we didn't run around much; we trained to hunt, and it was all very focused on the target. It was all for hunting, not combat. We rarely had combat." Tarkas explained. He looked around. "Hey, do we use our own arrows, or do they provide arrows for us?"

"They have arrows, but if you have your own, use them. That way, they can tell the difference and identify yours," Skolsav said.

"Alright then. This is my first archery competition outside of home, so it'll be interesting," Tarkas said.

"We'll see. Good luck to you," Skolsav said, patting him on the back.

They lined up in groups of five, and the first group shot their arrows. The highest score in each round would move on to the next round, and then the top five would compete. In case of a tie, one extra would move on. Tarkas was up, in front of Skolsav, so there was a chance they would meet in the finals. He drew his bow and aimed. In the formal seats, he noticed two women who appeared to be monarchs, along with a young, regal man sitting next to them. "Must be the royal family," he thought. "Good, I can catch them before they leave."

Tarkas shot the first arrow—bullseye. He shot again, and another bullseye, with the arrow landing right next to the first. Then he shot the third, making it three bullseyes. The crowd cheered for Tarkas. Skolsav was up next.

"Good job, you're going to give me a run for my money," Skolsav said.

Tarkas laughed and tried to approach the spectator section, but the man in the tunic from earlier stopped him. "Can't go there until the end—it's just the rules."

"Alright." Tarkas shrugged it off and watched as Skolsav also made three bullseyes.

When the round was done, Tarkas went over to Skolsav. "Good job."

"You're not the only one who can make it look easy," Skolsav said, patting Tarkas on the back.

Tarkas laughed, enjoying the competitive banter. It reminded him of being home, and he wondered if he could get used to this place.

Tarkas enjoyed watching the other archers shoot their arrows. There were a lot of skilled archers in the competition, all wearing the colors and clothes of their nations. Tarkas didn't recognize many of the colors. The world was a lot bigger than he could have ever imagined, and he wondered how many people were out there. He stood there blankly, leaning on one of the fence posts around the tournament grounds, lost in thought, until Skolsav gave him a pat on the back.

"Hey, our turn is up. You're not too tired, are you?" he teased.

Tarkas snapped back to reality. "I'm very alert and ready for this."

"Just so you know, I'm not going easy on you just because you're from out of town."

Tarkas laughed. "Wait, we're supposed to be trying? I could win this with my eyes closed."

This round of the competition had the final four stand in a row and aim, then count for the highest scores. They all shot their arrows. Tarkas was feeling good about getting another three bullseyes, then he looked at the others. They were all very close. He waited for the judges to determine the results.

"We have a tie!" the judge called out.

Tarkas and Skolsav turned to look at each other. "Now what?" Tarkas asked.

The judge came over and said. "Sudden death. You will shoot at your own targets—three more arrows."

Skolsav waved his hand. "No, one target. That way, one of us can't hit the same spot twice."

Tarkas nodded. "I agree. You can go first since you were last year's champion."

The judge looked at the two men who were certain about these rules. "Alright, if that's what you want. Go for it."

Skolsav shot his arrow and got an instant bullseye. "Ha, beat that! I've got this one!"

Tarkas stepped up and shot. His arrow wedged itself next to Skolsav's. "Looks like you'll have to shoot again."

He glared at Tarkas. "How are you getting so many bullseyes?"

"I haven't gotten any more than you. I think we're just equally matched," Tarkas replied.

Skolsav grabbed two of the generic bows and arrows, handing one set to Tarkas. "Let's use their equipment for this next shot."

Tarkas knew it was to give them a different feel, and maybe Skolsav suspected it was the bow. But Tarkas wasn't going to give up. The target was reset, and Tarkas noticed a sudden updraft in the wind. He recalculated how and when to shoot the arrow. He aimed, and *smack*—dead center, another bullseye.

Skolsav, distracted by his frustration, shot his arrow without considering the wind change and missed the center. He wasn't off by much, but enough to lose. He kicked the ground in frustration.

Tarkas patted him on the back. "You did fine. This was a great competition."

Skolsav took a deep breath and laughed. "Yeah, you gave me a run for my money. I just really wanted to win."

The judge came over and held up Tarkas's arm. "And the winner is Tarkas of the Crystal Caves!"

Tarkas waved to the crowd. The Queen and her family rose from their seats, clapped for Tarkas, and then soon left.

Tarkas moved to follow them but was held back by the referee. "Hold up, where are you going?"

"I wanted to talk to the monarch. I need to speak with her," Tarkas said.

"You can talk to her later when you go to collect your prize at the palace. Right now, you need to collect your token to take to her," the referee said.

Tarkas sighed. "Alright, I can wait."

Kaste arrived shortly after. "What's going on? The Queen left?"

"We'll see her in a bit. I have to collect my prize token," Tarkas said.

"Alright, I can wait," Kaste replied.

"Hey, mage, you didn't have anything to do with Tarkas winning, did you?" Skolsav asked.

Kaste rolled his eyes. "Hey, I stayed 200 feet away. I didn't do anything to alter the contest."

Tarkas found the comment odd, but he patted Skolsav on the back. "You shot well. We can shoot arrows again sometime. I swear I didn't cheat."

"I know you didn't. I just wish I had those 500 gold coins—my family could have used the money," Skolsav said.

"Come with me to the castle, and we'll talk more about this," Tarkas said as they collected their chips. They headed off toward the palace. "I come from a village that doesn't use currency. We had a trade deal with Centoria, so I'm still getting used to the whole concept of money."

"Well, my village doesn't use currency either. We trade our goods with the city here for extras, but I use the prize money to spend in the city and bring back supplies," Skolsav said as they walked to the palace.

Tarkas turned to Kaste. "How much money is needed to stay here? I don't really need it. We can give the prize money to Skolsav."

Kaste groaned. "Yeah, we can work something out if that's what you want."

When they arrived at the palace, Tarkas went straight up to the throne and knelt before the Queen. "Your Majesty, I have come to warn you of a great and powerful danger that is coming this way."

A look of concern crossed her face. "Don't you want your prize money?"

"I do, but I really need to talk to you about this first. That's why I'm in town. I've been staying at the Mages' College, and nothing is being done about this. I don't know if you've been notified."

Her eyes narrowed. "Dormir knows about this? And hasn't told me? Okay, now I'm interested."

Tarkas focused on the Queen and ignored everyone else in the room. "Your Majesty, I'm from the Crystal Caves outside of Centoria. There's an evil sorceress who is stealing magic from everywhere and trying to start a new world order. She and her crew have already wiped out my village and stolen magic from the cities west of here. She's coming here soon. My friends and I came here to warn you. We went to the Mages' College, and they said they contacted you, but when I didn't hear an update, Kaste and I came to check in."

The Queen raised her hand. "No need to explain further. I've dealt with Master Dormir for years—we don't get along. It's more than likely that he never sent a message to me. Once I've sorted out your prize money, I'll go with you to the Mages' College and get this resolved."

The royal guard handed Tarkas a bag containing 500 gold pieces and then gave Skolsav another bag with 250 gold pieces. While Tarkas was waiting for the Queen to get ready, he went over to Skolsav.

"Hey, I know I won the contest, but from what you've told me, your village needs the money more than I do. How about I give you the difference? I only entered the contest for fun. It wasn't something I was planning on winning," Tarkas said.

Skolsav looked at the gold coins in Tarkas's hand. "Is what you said true about the evil sorceress?"

"Why wouldn't it be?" Tarkas asked, surprised at his new friend's question.

"I'll take the money, and thank you, but I'll also help you. I have to return to my village soon, but while I'm here, I wouldn't mind helping," Skolsav said, taking the coins from Tarkas's hand.

Tarkas smiled and patted him on the shoulder. "Alright then, come with us."

They all made their way from the palace toward the Mages' College. When they arrived, Master Varucca rushed up to Tarkas. "Where were you? Your barbarian friend is going crazy looking for you!"

Tarkas laughed. "Sorry about that. Where is he?"

"He's in the kitchen. We calmed him down with food," Varucca said.

"Okay, go get Master Dormir and tell him to meet us there. The Queen wants to speak with him." Tarkas marched down to the food hall, not letting anyone stop him. When he got there, he saw Dorak eating a loaf of bread.

"Where have you been?" Dorak mumbled.

"Out, making friends, but someone had to get the Queen," Tarkas said.

"Tarkas, you're back! I told you not to leave the college—it's not safe out there," Master Dormir said.

Tarkas glared at him. "I can handle myself. You also told me you contacted the Queen, and, well, she never got your message."

Master Dormir looked over Tarkas's shoulder and saw the Queen standing there. He froze. "Your Majesty, it's nice to see you. I'm sorry you missed my messenger bird."

"Dormir, stop with the excuses. I know your undermining tricks, and I'm here to figure out how to protect my kingdom. You seem to be holding onto the only people with information about this threat."

Grandmaster Stellaris spoke up. "You worry too much, Navessa. Dormir was waiting for me to arrive so we could work on a plan together. And look, we've all met now, so we can work together."

The Queen glared at her. "Right. Well, then let's waste no time and sort this out."

"Not so fast. I also came here to speak with Tarkas." The Grandmaster looked at Tarkas for a moment, raised her hand, and brushed his hair aside from his face. "Oh, Tarkas, I'm so glad to have met someone like you."

Tarkas frowned. "What do you mean, someone like me? What am I?"

"I had to see it to believe it. I've only read about your type in books. Tarkas, you are a conduit and the key to winning this fight."

Tarkas and the Hidden Magic

"Tarkas is not a magic user!" Dorak shouted.

"We didn't say he was—that's not what a conduit is," Master Dormir said.

"I know what they are, and Tarkas is not one at all. He was tested—he is not a magic user!" Dorak snapped back.

"Dorak is right. I have no magic abilities," Tarkas said.

"What about your perfect aim?" Skolsav asked.

Tarkas chuckled. "I beat you fair and square. I've practiced my whole life to be a good archer. There's nothing I can't hit because of my skill, not because of magic."

"Tarkas, I understand this might be hard to hear, but since you've been here, there's been a power surge among the mages, and no one can explain it. There's something different about you," the Grandmaster said.

Dorak abruptly stood up. "No, you're wrong! Tarkas is not who you think he is. Now drop it!"

"What's the big deal if your friend is a conduit or not?" the Grandmaster asked.

"You don't know what you're talking about," Tarkas said. "Let's drop it for now and move on to the plan to stop Zara. We can do that without bringing my lineage into it, okay?"

They were all quiet for a moment. Then the Queen spoke up. "Do we know where her base is and when she plans to attack?"

Kaste spoke up. "No, but I think Orph, that's his name, knows—the new apprentice. We saw him talking to her before we left. They were by the supply door."

"That's how you two got out!" Master Dormir glared at Kaste. "I think you're mistaken. He has nothing to do with her."

"I was there. I heard it too. He isn't lying. Want the truth? Bring this apprentice here now and ask him, because he was making a deal to hand me over to Zara," Tarkas said.

Master Dormir sighed and turned to one of the mages at another table. "Go get Orph; he's needed."

The mage finished his bite of food and said. "Right away, sir." He got up and headed off.

They stood there in silence for a moment. Then the Queen spoke up. "I want the travelers to stay outside the Mages' College. I want them working with my man-at-arms unit to defend the city."

"No, these enemies are magic users. They should be fought with magic," Master Dormir said.

"Your college isn't the only place that needs protecting, unless you're offering to help me," the Queen said. She turned to look at Kaste. "You're a magic user. What side are you on?"

Kaste laughed awkwardly. "Well, I'm on the side that gets my brother back. I think Dormir only lets me stay because he has to by mage law."

Dormir yawned. "Kaste, you were always a troublemaker."

"See what I mean?" Kaste said. "In short, my Queen, I will help you."

Before Master Dormir could say anything in rebuttal, Orphj and the other mage returned. "You sent for me?"

"Yes, what do you know about a sorceress named Zara?" Dormir asked.

Orph looked nervous. "Nothing... who is that?"

Dorak grabbed his axe and pointed it at the young mage's throat. "I won't ask you again. What do you know, and what does she want with Tarkas?"

Sweat rolled down his forehead as the axe grazed his throat. "Alright, I'll tell you what I know. Gosh, has anyone ever told you barbarians that you're scary?"

Dorak snarled. "Good. Now start talking."

"It started about a year ago. Some of the mages would sneak out to have some fun, and then we met this sorceress, Zara. She was lovely and enchanting, and she promised to teach us magic they didn't teach in the academy. That's what happened to your brother, Kaste. He fell in love with her, but she didn't teach us much—just helped us develop our magic. I think she was just scouting for new recruits. Their base is in the mountains. I can show you. I didn't know she was bad—I didn't mean to get in trouble."

"Why are you still helping her? And why does she want me?" Tarkas asked.

"I don't know. I thought she left me alone, but then the other day, when you saw me, she came to the supply door. I agreed to help because I don't want her mad at me. Have you seen her mad?" Orph said.

"Did she say anything else about why? Because she had me once and let me go," Tarkas asked.

"I have no idea, but I can send her a message to tell her to come and get you, if that will help."

They all smiled, and then the Queen spoke up. "Send her a message and show me where in the mountains her base is, and we'll set a trap for her. Tarkas, I hope you don't mind being the bait?"

"I can't say I enjoy it, but I like the idea. I'm also not too worried about it—I know someone in her gang," Tarkas said.

"Good, then let's make a plan back at the castle, with the guards there," the Queen said.

"Hold up, why not make the plan here right now?" Master Dormir said.

"Because I don't trust you. But if you want, we can all go to the palace and talk about it there, and you can join. It's also getting late—it's not a good time to be walking back and forth. Let's meet up tomorrow morning."

They exchanged glances and nodded in agreement. "Alright then, we'll meet at the palace in the morning to talk about the attack," Dormir said.

"What if we don't wait until morning and talk here tonight?" Dorak asked. "I'm willing to stay up—anything to make progress."

The Queen sighed. "I am too, but we might hear from Zara by morning. It's getting dark, and my man-at-arms should be present. We'll be more clear-headed in the morning. If you want to come back to the castle with me, you're all welcome."

"I think I'll head back with you," Dorak said. "I want to be right where the action is happening."

"I won't be staying here tonight either—I have a room at the inn now," Tarkas said.

"Tarkas, before you leave, I wish to have a talk with you," Grandmaster Stellira said.

"Um, sure, I guess," Tarkas said.

"Tarkas, I'll wait for you until your conversation is done," Dorak said.

Tarkas turned to Skolsav. "Sorry about all this running around. Is it okay if you stay an extra day?"

"I'm in town for the week, so as long as I'm back in my village with supplies before the winter hits, I'll be fine. I can stay a few more days. I'll head back to the inn with you—it's getting dark, and it'll be easier to see with everyone," Skolsav responded.

"Alright I'll go talk to the grandmaster and then we can head out." Tarkas turned to her. "alright I'm ready to go."

"I'm coming with you," Kaste said. "I understand a lot of this magic stuff.

"if he is going I'm going to." Dorak said

"Alright, follow me." Grandmaster Stellira guided Tarkas and the group to a small office at the top of the stone steps. The office was not unlike Master Dormir's, filled with jars and books. She sat down in her chair. "Do you have any questions for me?"

"Well, yeah. What is a conduit, and why would you think that I am one?" Tarkas asked.

"Tarkas, what do you know about your birth parents?"

"Nothing. I was adopted," Tarkas said.

"Tarkas, have you ever been close to magic users?"

He let out a sigh. "There was one in my village—Airis. He's the one working with Zara. We were close."

"Did he ever notice a power boost when you were near?" she asked.

"I do," Kaste spoke up. All eyes turned to him. "Since I've met him, my powers have been growing more and more."

"I tried as a child to do magic, but it never worked. Airis tried to get me to do spells as a kid, and nothing would happen. Is this just a case of inspiration?" Tarkas asked.

Dorak cut in. "See? No magic. You're wrong."

Stellira groaned. "I'm not wrong. Tarkas, can I have some of your blood? Just a couple of drops."

Tarkas held out his hand. "I guess if this will settle it."

She took a pin from her shelf, pricked Tarkas's hand, and dropped a few drops of blood into a vial. She then moved the blood toward Kaste, and they all watched as the blood began to glow and shimmer. When she moved it toward Dorak, the blood returned to normal. She then held the blood toward herself, and it glowed slightly, but not as much as it had with Kaste. "I think that proves it."

Tarkas narrowed his eyes in confusion. "How am I this conduit that you say I am?"

She turned to Dorak. "When he was found, was it at the base of Mount Elderon?"

Dorak glared at her. "So I've been told. I wasn't there, but I remember my parents talking about it when I was older."

"I thought so. You're the son of the gods," she said.

Everyone's eyes widened. "What are you talking about? That's not possible," Tarkas said.

"I've been around for a long time. The gods normally can't have children, but almost 30 years ago, one was born. It was a shock, and they voted to get rid of the child because the child would be alone, and it was seen as a bad omen. My guess is, if you're here, your mother loved you and left you on the mountain. You're an anomaly, the only child born from them in hundreds of years."

Tarkas sighed. "This is a lot to take in... Wow. Does being a child of the gods make me a conduit?"

"Conduits don't normally exist—they're not typical. You bridge the gap between all types of magic but can never use it," she paused. "I bet the gods knew who you were when your friend brought you there.

The fountain is unfiltered, and no normal person survives drinking that water, let alone being brought back to life."

Tarkas turned to Dorak. "Is this why you took me to the gods when I died?"

Dorak sighed. "I was desperate to continue this journey, and I wasn't going to do it alone. I took a chance that they would help you—I didn't know what would happen."

Tarkas took a deep breath. "Alright then, what does this mean?"

"Well, we wanted you to stay at the Mages' College so we can study this, because it's an anomaly," she said. "But this is probably why Zara wants you."

"Well, I don't want to stay here much longer. I prefer to stay in town, away from magic," Tarkas said. "I will decide where I am staying after the meeting tomorrow."

Grandmaster Stellira nodded. "Alright, then."

Tarkas went with Kaste and Skolsav back to the inn. He wanted to sleep and forget the day—it was a lot for his mind to process. But when they walked into the bar, there was a loud cheer congratulating them for winning the archery contest. Tarkas knew right then that there would be no sleep with all this noise, so he joined in the drinking. Drinking would help him forget what he had just learned, and they drank into the night.

He turned to Kaste before he was too drunk. "Hey, is there a way to make sure we'll be up in the morning for the meeting?"

Kaste finished a sip of his beer. "Yeah, I'll do a spell to make sure we wake up." Then he went back to his beer.

They all drank and sang songs into the night, and for the first time in a long while, Tarkas forgot about his worries and just enjoyed himself.

In the morning, they were all awakened by the bartender throwing a bucket of water on their heads. "Wake up!" the bartender shouted.

Tarkas opened his eyes, rubbed them, and looked at the light coming through the window. He shook Kaste. "You said you were going to do a wake-up spell."

Kaste brushed back his long black hair. "I must've forgotten, but we should be fine. Let's get up and go."

"I don't care where you go, I need to clean up the bar for the morning," the bartender said.

Tarkas shook Skolsav awake, and soon they all gathered their things and made their way to the palace.

Dorak was by the doors. "I was about to head out and find you."

"Dorak, I can take care of myself. And we're here on time," Tarkas said.

They all went into the meeting room and sat at the round table in the center of the stone room.

"Alright, is everyone here?" the Queen asked.

Tarkas looked around and saw Kaste, Skolsav, Master Dormir, Grandmaster Stellira, Lira, Kaley, Mage Orph, Kal, the Queen consort, and Prince Voylin.

The Queen turned to look at Kal. "Prince Kal, it's so nice to finally meet you."

Kal raised an eyebrow at her. "It's nice to meet you too. But how do you know me?"

"You're a Prince of Centoria. I know a lot about you, so I'm guessing your father sent you as an envoy?"

Kal shook his head. "I'm no longer a prince. My father allowed me to come, but I've renounced my claim to the throne."

"Well, that is good to know. We can talk more about it afterward, but I'm still glad you're here." She turned to the rest of the table. "Mage Orph, did you manage to get in touch with Zara?"

"Yes, I did. She's willing to meet to trade for Tarkas," he said.

"We're not giving up Tarkas. He stays with us!" Dorak shouted.

The Queen raised her hand. "We haven't decided that yet."

"No, I want to go back. Can someone put a tracking spell on me? Then we can find out where her base is. She wants me alive, so she won't kill me. Maybe I can get some info out of her."

"I just want her dead, as quickly as possible," Dorak said. "By tribal law, she must be executed."

"Zara is a mage who has hurt our mages. We must deal with her," Dormir said.

"I see that we have many governing forces here. Alright, Prince Kal, what would your father's stance be on this?" the Queen asked.

"He was comfortable with Dorak handling it, and it's my choice to join Dorak on this journey. So, I must align myself with the Crystal Caves," Kal said.

"My Queen, asked for our magic artifacts back and is not concerned about what happens to her since Queen Keltrice blames us." Captain Kaley said.

"Is that so?" The Queen turned to Dormir. "Zara threatens my kingdom as much as she threatens your school. Those students were also residents. If she's targeting my kingdom's magic users, then I need to take action."

"Do we have the power to stop her?" Lira asked. They all paused for a moment to think before she continued. "The last few times we've faced her, we couldn't do much damage. This might be our only chance to fight her again."

They all pondered what she said. Then Tarkas spoke up. "That's why I want to be captured—to find out what she wants from me. She had me once, so why does she want me back? I say put a tracking spell on me or something. Come get me, and make sure you're not followed so you can surprise her. Also, you can get a feel for her magical imprint."

The room was silent. They all looked at each other and nodded.

"Alright, and when we do the surprise attack, we kill her," Dorak said.

The Queen raised her hand. "Now wait. She may be wanted for death in your lands, but if captured, she's on my land, and we'll deal with her under my laws. However, I will consider yours once we capture her. So we need to take her alive."

Dorak grumbled. "Fine."

The Queen turned to Mage Orph. "Send another message to Mistress Zara and tell her where to find Tarkas. Preferably today."

Mage Orph said a few words, blew into his fingers, and conjured a magical bird with a clear, crystalized appearance. "I'll send the message from here." He took out the pre-written letter from last night, attached it to the magic bird's foot, and released it from the window. "Magic birds travel faster than real ones."

"Where did you say we were meeting up?" Tarkas asked.

"At the service door of the Mage College, where she wanted to meet the first time."

The Queen turned to Kaste. "I have other duties to attend to, so I'm counting on you to make sure no magical shenanigans take place."

She looked at Kal. "You and my son, Prince Veylin, are responsible for upholding the laws of Alwyndia. Is that understood?"

Kal nodded. "Yes, Your Highness."

"Meeting dismissed," the Queen said. They all stood up and left the room.

Tarkas went over to Skolsav. "Hey, I'm sorry if that meeting was boring for you. But I appreciate you coming."

"Well, I'm in town for a few days. I'll be there when we get you back, but I'm going to head to town and place some orders for my village." Skolsav patted Tarkas on the back. "Take care."

Tarkas patted him back before they parted ways. "I will, thank you."

"Tarkas, I hope you know what you're doing. I don't want you getting hurt," Dorak said.

"I do, and you'll get your vengeance. I'm just going to be the bait," Tarkas said.

They all made their way to the cargo entrance and waited for Zara to show. Master Dormir put a magical charm on Tarkas's leather armor. Kaste gave Tarkas an enchanted kiss to track him without Dormir noticing. Mage Orph bound Tarkas's hands and waited with him by the entrance. The others stayed hidden inside the tower. A couple of hours passed before a lady in a black cloak appeared.

"Do you have him?" she asked.

Orph pushed Tarkas forward. "Here he is. Where's my cut?"

"Where's his bow?" she asked.

Orph handed her Tarkas's red bow. "Right here."

"Good." She took the bow and handed him a bag with 25 gold pieces in it. "Here you go." She placed her hand on Tarkas's shoulder. "Come with me."

She took Tarkas away. They mounted a black horse with glowing red eyes. The horse rode a few feet before flying into the air. Kaste, who was watching, whispered a few words into his hand, blew into them, and released a more natural-looking magic bird, which flew after them.

"Why did you do that? We have him tracked," Orph asked.

"Those aren't strong enough from this distance to track her. She didn't ride all the way there, so we can't follow her directly. This bird will give us a bird's-eye view of where she's headed," Kaste explained.

"So now we just wait?" Dorak said, coming up behind Kaste.

Kaste tensed at the sound of Dorak's voice behind him and quickly turned around. "Please don't sneak up on me. And yes, we wait."

"I don't like this plan," Dorak said.

"You don't like anything," Kaley added.

Dorak turned to Kaley and snarled. "I don't like the idea of this plan. That witch is not to be trusted."

Dorak Uneased

Dorak picked up his battle axe and prepared for battle. He walked out of the Mages' College, but as he reached the gates, he was stopped by Kaley.

She stood in front of him and raised her hand to stop him. "Where do you think you're going?"

"I'm tired of waiting for this attack. Let's just get going—who knows what they're doing to Tarkas," Dorak said, staring down at her.

She stared back at him. "It's been one day. We're supposed to wait three for the surprise attack. We found out her base is only half a day from here, so we don't want to rush in. We need the element of surprise."

"I don't care. Her judgment is overdue. I can take her," Dorak said.

"Please, just wait. Go train with us and get better. We all miss Tarkas and are worried about him, but he'll be okay," Kaley said.

Dorak grunted and went back to the college.

Kal lay in bed next to Kleo and kissed her on the lips. "I missed you."

Kleo laughed. "It was only two days. We don't have to see each other all the time."

Kal played with her long hair in his hands. "I know that, but it's so nice to meet someone who knows my culture and understands the diaspora I'm feeling. I can talk to you about it. I know I have my cousin, but she's never lived away."

She kissed him on the cheek. "I really appreciate that. It's nice to have someone to talk to. Maybe we could meet up outside of work, and I can show you more of our customs."

"I would love that," Kal said.

"Great. Do you want to do it tomorrow?" she asked.

Kal let out a sigh. "No, I can't. I have to leave tomorrow for the attack—a sort of rescue mission for Tarkas. We had to wait three days before going after him, and if we leave tomorrow, we'll be there on time. I don't know when I'll be back, but I will be back. It should be simple. But when I return, I'd love to meet up."

She gave him a hug. "Please stay safe. I'd hate for anything bad to happen to you."

"I'll be fine. I'm skilled and have seen my fair share of battles. This one will be easy—it's just a couple of magic users. Nothing should happen." He noticed her worry and gave her a kiss. "I promise you, I'll be back."

They embraced and kissed passionately on the bed. Then the madam knocked on the door frame. "Time's up. I'd normally bill you, Kal, for another hour, but she has a client and needs to get cleaned up."

They broke their embrace. "Well, I've got to go. Take care, and I'll see you soon." He got out of bed and put on his clothes.

"Take care," she said.

"Come on, Lira, you've got to do better than that!" Kaley called out, swinging her sword at Lira again.

Lira blocked the sword with her shield. "I'm trying, but why does it feel like the more I train, the weaker I get?"

Kaley swung her sword again. "You just need more practice. Keep going—you'll get better."

Lira tripped and fell. "I think I'm done for now. We're leaving later today; how about we rest?"

Kaley walked over and helped her up. "Alright, we've been working hard. You can take a break until we need to leave."

Lira went over to one of the benches in the courtyard and sat down. She rubbed her sore leg and let out a sigh of defeat.

Kaley sat down next to her. "I know you want to be a fighter, but this is all new to you. Maybe you're not cut out for it."

Lira frowned. "No, I can do it. I'm just getting weaker, and it's getting harder. But it should be getting easier, not harder."

"Your form is getting better, but your endurance is dropping. My guess is you're tired. Take it easy until we need to go. Maybe one of the mages has a potion or spell that can help you recover faster."

Lira smiled. "Yeah, I'll go ask Kaste and see if he has something. I really want to do this."

"Hey, I want you to know you have a lot of potential, and I'm glad you're showing initiative," Kaley said. "Just give it time."

Lira went into the Mages' College and looked around for Kaste. She found him in one of the towers, alone, tossing a book off the table.

She picked it up and put it back on the desk. "Hey, don't damage the book—it isn't yours."

He stopped and looked at her. "Sorry, I'm just frustrated. I'm trying to prepare with my magic, but I'm feeling a power withdrawal from Tarkas not being here. I've never had one, so I didn't realize the 'come down' would mess with my head so much. But what can I help you with?"

Lira sat next to Kaste in the other chair by the desk. "I've been training with Kaley, but I'm getting more and more fatigued when I train. I don't know what's going on."

Kaste walked over to Lira and waved his hand around her. "How long has this been happening? Do you have any other pains?"

"A little muscle soreness, but nothing else. It's been happening for the past week."

Kaste pulled out a vial and a needle. "Can I take some blood to see if I can find something?"

"Sure." Lira held out her hand.

"No, roll up your sleeve. The arm is easier," Kaste said as he moved closer.

She rolled up her puffy sleeve to reveal her bare arm. Kaste pricked her bicep, taking a small sample of blood. He placed a cloth over her arm to stop the bleeding, then took the vial over to the potion table. He mixed a drop of blood with one of the vials from the shelf and frowned when the blood turned blue. He then took another vial, mixed in more blood, and it turned blue again. He tried a third vial, and the blood turned green. He let out a deep sigh and turned back toward Lira.

"Have you had any recent weight gain?"

Lira shook her head. "Nothing noticeable."

"Well, I'm not a doctor, but I think you have a virus—not a regular one. It's too soon to be anything else, and no one else is reporting symptoms. So, my best guess is: did you and Merv do anything when you brought him food?"

Her face blushed. "Well, we talked for a bit."

Kaste rolled his eyes. "I took you to a brothel, and you've seen my appetite—you can be open with me."

She sighed. "Yes, one of the days I spent more time with Merv. Do you think I caught a fish disease?"

"I think you got something more than that, but I'm no doctor," Kaste laughed. "The good news is I don't think it's contagious. I can give you some pills to help with the blood pressure, but you should take it easy."

Her eyes widened. "Are you saying you think I'm pregnant?"

Kaste shrugged. "I'm not sure. I think it's highly unlikely, but it's something to keep an eye on. You should see a real doctor. I checked—it has his energy patterns. I can give you something for the symptoms. He might have just implanted some kind of magic in you. But if you gain weight or start growing fins or scales, let me know, and we'll revisit this." He went over to the potion shelf and grabbed a vial. "This one should do the trick." He handed it to her.

She took it hesitantly. "Um, thank you."

"Don't worry—I won't tell anyone anything you don't want me to," Kaste said, sitting back at the desk.

She leaned over. "So, are you still upset because of the power drop, or is it because you miss Tarkas?"

Kaste groaned and glared at her. "You got your cure—you don't have to stay."

"Like you said, we all know you and Tarkas are an item. So, spill the beans."

He sighed. "I don't know, and that's what's bothering me. Simple as that—I don't know what I miss more. All I know is we need to get him and my brother back. Then maybe I'll be less grumpy."

"So, you weren't always grumpy?" Lira asked.

"Nope. Life just keeps finding ways to throw curveballs at me. I never stay happy for long."

A look of remorse crossed her face. "Well, I hope you find happiness."

She got up from the chair and was heading out of the room when Kaste began to speak. "Plock is my twin brother. We were inseparable when we were kids. I was always the troublemaker, and he would bail me out. Our parents couldn't stand the trouble we got into. They died when we were teens. Mom got sick first, and Dad spent what little money he had sending us to the Mages' College because we were magic users. We went, and when we came back for the holidays, he had died of something medical, and the house had been robbed. That house—the one you saw—Is the one I grew up in. I never got along with Master Dormir—he never got my sense of humor. My brother and I were too much for him. Eventually, I went back to our parents' house and got a job using my magic for hire. My brother and I would see each other often, but then one day, he came by and said, 'I met an amazing sorceress, and I'm running off with her.' I argued with him, not because he met someone, but because he didn't have a plan to come back. He was just going to leave. I need him back. We're twins…" His rambling trailed off.

Lira went over and gave Kaste a hug from behind. "I'm sorry you're going through all of this."

"I just need more time to myself. I'll be ready to fight and get him back," Kaste said.

Dorak was up at the crack of dawn ready to fight axe in hand and Brimstone his hell pig by his side. He waited at the bottom of the hill for everyone to arrive. Soon, the band of heroes appeared, followed by Prince Veylin, who showed up with an army of 100 soldiers. Dorak went over to the prince. "What is this? We don't need an army to fight her—we just need my axe!" He held up his red axe.

The prince looked down from his horse. "How many times have you tried that, and it didn't work? My mother, the queen, doesn't doubt your skill but wants to ensure we're well-prepared."

Dorak snarled at the prince. "It's a waste of effort, but you can stay back as reinforcements." He headed to the front of the line and turned to Kaste. "You got enough magic for this?"

Kaste glared at him. "Magic isn't about an amount; it's about endurance. And yes, I've got enough."

"You better. Lead the way," Dorak said, then turned to the rest of them. "Follow us!" Dorak mounted Brimstone and rode off, following the path to Zara's lair that Kaste and the other mages had mapped out.

They traveled for a while, Dorak focused on the road ahead. Eventually, Skolsav rode up next to Dorak on his horse. "You don't talk much, do you?"

Dorak glanced at Skolsav, then back to the path. "What's there to talk about?"

"Fair," Skolsav said. "I was just wondering—what's your plan after all this is done and you've dealt with Zara?"

Dorak glared at Skolsav. "I'll deal with that once it's done. What's your connection to Tarkas?"

"He bested me in the archery contest in town and shared his prize money with me to help my village. He's a good man, and I promised to help him with this fight before I return to my village," Skolsav explained.

Dorak grunted. "What rank do you hold in your village?"

"My village has a council where one person from each trade speaks for the others. As the best archer, I speak for the hunters, but there's no single chief. There's a leader for the hunters, fishers, crafters, farmers, and builders. How did the system work in your village?"

"Chiefs. The strongest would fight to be the leader, and once we had a chief, it went to his child, who could either be accepted or challenged. We're protectors, and strength is our biggest virtue," Dorak said.

"Not bad. Was Tarkas the best archer in your village?"

"One of the best. He didn't get any of the strength gifts from the waters—he got high intelligence and worked twice as hard as a kid to keep up with the rest of us. Archery was where he excelled. He practiced twice as hard every day," Dorak said, showing signs of remorse.

"You really miss him?" Skolsav asked.

Dorak gave him a side glare. "He's my best friend and like a brother to me. I'm not going to let any harm come to him. He's the only family I have left. His safety is highly important to me."

"I understand," Skolsav said. "I'll ask again, what are your plans after you defeat this witch?"

Dorak was silent for a moment. "I'll think about that when it happens. Until then, I have a job to do."

"STOP!" Kaste called out. They were a few hours into the trip and nearly half way there.

Dorak halted his hell pig. "why are we stopping?"

"I have lost Tarkas's signal," Kaste said.

"What does this mean mage!" Dorak's eyes boiled with rage.

"Someone has wiped off his tracking I put on. I just lost his location. But we still know where the cave is." Kaste said.

Dorak reached over towards Kaste who was on his gryphon and grabbed his collar. "is he dead? Did we wait to long to rescue him?"

Kaste struggled to get out of Dorak's grip. "No, I don't think so, I just can no longer track him. If he were dead the tracking would still be on, someone purposely removed it. It's safe to assume that they know were coming."

"I knew we shouldn't have waited." Dorak let go of Kaste, and adjusted himself on his beast. "well then no time to waste, hurry up let's go!" Then he road off faster ahead of the group. They all followed ahead Dorak picking up the pace.

Tarkas in Chains

Tarkas awoke, bound in chains to the wall of a stone room. He struggled, attempting to free his hands.

"You're awake," Zara said, stepping into the room. "How are you feeling?"

Tarkas pulled at one of his chains. "Not happy I'm bound. Why do you want me? You had me before."

"I am a woman of my word, and I traded you for the stone before, but I still need you." She stepped closer, standing in front of him. "I noticed an energy surge when you were here, and I know that Grandmaster Stellia arrived once you did. I want to know what she said to you."

"Why don't you ask her?" Tarkas replied.

She grabbed his neck. "Don't be difficult. This won't be pleasurable for you."

He gulped, struggling to breathe as her hand tightened. "Alright, I'll tell you." He felt her grip ease. "She thinks I'm a conduit and that I might be the son of the gods."

She paused, staring into his eyes, then brushed his hair back. "You look so much like your father. I can't believe it's actually you. You lived. I knew she wouldn't let you die."

Tarkas frowned. "What do you mean?"

"Did she tell you anything else?" she asked, examining his features.

"I might be the son of the gods, that's all I know."

She brushed his hair back and stepped away. "You are, and I'm your aunt. Your father is my brother, and your birth was a total anomaly. We all voted for you to be put to death. How did your mother save you?"

"From what I've been told, I was left in the woods at the base of the mountain, and Gorak's hunting party found me. But you're my aunt?"

She sighed and sat in the room's chair. "I didn't expect this. I thought you were just a source of energy; I didn't realize you were my nephew—the only one I've seen in close to a thousand years. When the fountain was discovered, our crops grew strong. But when our well water ran dry and Zelma drank from the fountain, they lived, and we began using the water more." She took a deep breath. "Within a day, the village was sick or dying. It was horrible. Twelve of us survived, and we vowed to prevent others from making the same mistake. But as time went on, we noticed we didn't die or age. And no children were born. When you turn a hundred and haven't gotten pregnant, you assume you can't. Eventually, we found the Crystal Caves, but we saw a couple of travelers drinking from it. They didn't die; they gained abilities, so we asked them to stay and protect the caves so no one else would be harmed by the waters. That's how your tribe was born. From there, I watched the seasons change, people grow, have families, and die. Then finally, Wella announced she was pregnant with my brother's child. We had no idea how this happened, and we had tried breeding with mortals. You were a miracle. We all tried to see if we could have children again, but none of us were as lucky. Once you were born, we had a meeting and decided, since you would grow and die with no other children around, you were to be put to death. I wasn't there for what happened next. Your mother must have snuck you out in the middle of the night. Makes sense why she saved you again when your friend brought you to her."

Tarkas listened in amazement and intrigue as Zara told the tale. "So, you gods aren't really creator gods? I always grew up believing you were watching over us. And you thought it was best to kill me? Isn't that counterproductive? Wouldn't you think I might reach maturity and not die? Why are you turning your back on the people you swore to protect?"

"Because sometimes people are just tired of the way things are!" She rushed over and slapped him. "You weren't there. You have no idea what it's like to live this long and see what I've seen! Don't you judge me!"

Tarkas tensed, failing to shift away. "Sorry, I'm just confused. What do you need from me, then?"

She took a deep breath and calmed down. "I knew you were a magic user, and well, most of us are magic users, but I had no idea at the time what type you were. It makes sense now why Cashper would have wanted you gone. Do you know what a conduit is?"

Tarkas shook his head. "Not really. Airis was the only magic user I grew up with."

She sighed. "Yes, because of Bernor. He couldn't control his powers and burned down the village once, so Chief Sornak put restrictions on magic users. But you are a conduit, which is different. You are a mix of magic user and non-magic user. You can siphon magic out of something and place it somewhere else, boosting the magic of people around you."

"So, you want me as a power boost?" Tarkas asked, guessing the grim purpose she had in mind.

"There are many types of magic in the world, and they cannot be mixed. But with a conduit, you can drain energy from one type and transfer it to another. You are what I've been looking for." She ran a hand through his hair. "You are going to work for me now."

Tarkas wriggled his arms in the chains. "And you think I'll work for you because you chained me up?"

She laughed. "No, you'll work for me because I have your lover, Airis, on my side. I know all about your special bond now."

Tarkas paused, contemplating. Part of him cared for Airis, unable to forget their years together, but there was also the betrayal—Airis faking his death, abandoning him, selling out, and murdering their families. Still, he preferred Airis's control to Zara's. "Oh yeah, I would love to see him again."

She grinned and headed to the door. "Good, then I'll send him your way."

Airis walked into the room, and Zara handed him the key to Tarkas's chains before leaving. Airis looked at Tarkas and went right over to him. "It's really nice to see you again." He leaned in and kissed Tarkas on the lips. "I missed you, and I'm glad you're back."

"It's good to be back, and I would enjoy it more if I weren't chained up in Zara's room. Could you loosen these chains, and maybe we could go somewhere else?" Tarkas jingled the chains on his arms.

Airis kissed Tarkas's neck. "I think it's sexy, you in these chains, but we can move this to my room." He took the key out of his pocket and unlocked Tarkas's chains. He watched as Tarkas rubbed his wrists and stretched his arms before presenting him with a set of shackles.

"What are these for?" Tarkas asked, stretching his arms.

"I can't let you walk out of here unbound. So, stretch your arms, but you've got to wear these." Airis held them out.

Tarkas glared at him. "You don't trust me?"

"It's not about trust—it's the fact that until we have your full loyalty, we need to keep you where we can see you." Airis opened one of the cuffs.

Tarkas conceded and held out his hands. "If this is the way it has to be, then so be it."

Airis put the shackles on his hands and locked them. "Follow me." They walked down the cave's hallways until they reached a wooden door at the end.

"What's this place?" Tarkas asked.

"It's my room," Airis paused. "Oh, you mean the cave. It's an old mine, so there are lots of rooms."

They entered the room, and Airis locked the door behind him. He took Tarkas over to the small bed, sat him down, and kissed him. "I missed you so much. I'm glad you're back."

Tarkas tried to move his hands to embrace him. "My hands are bound. Could we maybe fix that?"

"I like them on you; it's sexy." He paused. "But I can do this." He took the key from his pocket, unlocked one hand, and hooked the empty cuff onto the bedpost. "Is that better?"

Tarkas stretched his arm. "It's better."

Airis began taking off his black leather mage robes. "I'm so glad you decided to come back."

"Well, how could I stay away?" Tarkas said, a hint of hesitation in his tone.

Airis finished undressing and then climbed on top of Tarkas. "You're still dressed. Let me help you with that." He kissed his way down Tarkas's body, removing his leather archer's armor as he went.

Tarkas caressed Airis's face. "So, this is how it's going to be."

Airis lifted his head. "Well, of course! What part of 'I missed you' didn't you get?"

"Sorry, it's just been a bit jarring getting here," Tarkas said, feeling used but playing along to avoid suspicion. He thought back to when he and Airis were teens. "I missed you too."

For a few moments, they were one, the pain of the past fading as they lived in the moment. Afterward, Airis lay on his back and sighed.

Tarkas, noticing something was amiss, asked. "Is something wrong?"

Airis let out another sigh. "I love being with you, and I love you, but that time didn't feel like it usually does. It felt... lackluster. It's hard to explain."

Tarkas paused, wondering if it had something to do with him being a conduit. "Well, I am chained up. Maybe that's why it didn't feel right?"

"No, that part was hot—that wasn't it." He paused and sat up. "It just didn't feel the same. I'm happy to be with you again, but I don't know..."

Tarkas continued wondering if it had to do with his conduit powers. 'What if Airis got a power boost from me before and didn't this time?' Tarkas wasn't sure how his powers really worked. He caressed Airis's leg. "I'm probably just tired. Believe me, I really enjoyed being with you." He knew he was lying but looked deeply into Airis's eyes, trying to convince him that he loved him and no other. Airis began to smile and leaned down to kiss Tarkas. "There's the man I love." He got up and started getting dressed. "I'm going to go get our dinner. I'll be back."

As soon as Airis left and closed the door, Tarkas began to cry. He felt used and lost, realizing nothing could be restored from his past with Airis. He had to learn to use his powers and regain control. He felt dirty for what he was doing but knew he needed the information that only Zara could provide. 'If she wants me to help her, she has to show me how to use my powers.'

A while later, Airis returned with some food and handed a bowl to Tarkas. He sat on one end of the bed and ate his meal alongside Tarkas. "So, what happened after I left the tribe?"

Tarkas put his bowl down on the bedside table. "I was sad for the longest time. Your mother missed you. She had a big fight with Gorak over it, and we all mourned for you. But then life went on."

"Did you move on?" he asked.

Tarkas felt nervous about mentioning Kaste but honestly replied. "There wasn't anyone else in the tribe I connected with quite like you. Did you?"

"No, I didn't," he said. "I wish I could have taken you with me. But hey, fate brought us back together, and now we can be together." He put his bowl aside and leaned over to kiss Tarkas.

Tarkas, overwhelmed with feelings of loss and never fully recovering from Airis's absence, felt his emotions flood back. They began passionately making out. Things were getting heated when a scream came from outside the room.

Tarkas stopped. "What was that?"

Airis rolled his eyes. "That's Zara and Plock. They're just... doing what we were doing."

Tarkas paused. "We don't sound like that, do we? I never thought about how it sounds to others."

Airis kissed Tarkas. "We don't sound like that, but if noise is going to be an issue, I could gag you?"

"Ugh, no thanks. The shackles are enough. Can we maybe take it off? Or hook it onto my ankle?" Tarkas pleaded.

"I'm not supposed to take it off, but I suppose I can." He paused, considering, then snapped his fingers, casting a purple glow on the door's lock. "There we go."

Tarkas raised an eyebrow. "What was that?"

"A magic lock on the door so only I can unlock it." He took the key out of his pocket and unlocked Tarkas's shackles. "Feel better?"

Tarkas rubbed his wrist. "Thanks for that. Those were really uncomfortable."

Airis leaned in and started kissing Tarkas's shoulders and neck. "Are you ready for bed?"

Tarkas kissed him back. "I am now."

In the morning, Tarkas was awoken by a knock at the door. He shook Airis awake. "Airis, you locked the door, and someone's there."

Airis rolled over, zapping the door's lock to unlock it, then rolled back onto the bed.

The door opened, and Tarkas used the one blanket to cover them as best he could. Zara entered the room. She walked over to the bed and nudged Airis with her foot. "Airis, I know you've been left in charge of Tarkas, but I need to borrow him for a bit. I promise to return him in one piece."

Airis rolled over, giving Tarkas room to get up. Tarkas started dressing. Zara went up to him before his shirt was on, touching his necrotic wounds. "You still haven't fully healed?"

He shook his head. "No, but they aren't getting worse."

"Good to know." She headed to the door. "Follow me."

Tarkas finished putting on his armor and followed Zara down to a lower level in the mine, to a large open area. "I'm going to teach you how to use your powers today."

"All right, where do we begin?"

She went over to a pile of rocks, selecting one that was red and warm, and handed it to him. "Drain this rock of its power."

He held the stone, feeling it resonate with energy. "How?"

She picked up a stone for herself and held it in her hand. "Start by feeling the energy of the stone, then try to absorb the energy."

Tarkas held the stone in his hand and thought about how he didn't want to hurt it. Soon, the rock started to glow even brighter.

"Stop that! You're giving it more power. You're leaking energy—you need to drain some of it," Zara commanded.

Tarkas tried to shift his focus, feeling Zara begin to get on his nerves, and directed that irritation into the stone. The stone started to lose its color and faded to the grey of most common rocks.

Zara smiled. "Good, it worked. Now, here's another stone. Put the power into this one."

Tarkas began to think that his power might be controlled by his emotions. He took the other rock from Zara, and soon it began to glow a vibrant green.

"Yes! My theory was correct! You can transfer any energy into another. This is amazing." Zara grinned and handed him another red rock. "Now, try it while you're holding both."

Tarkas took a deep breath and tried to focus first on one rock, then the other. Within moments, the power started to shift colors back and forth, flashing between his hands. "Wow, I never thought I could do this."

"You can do so much more. Drain the two rocks of their power now and put their energy into me." She took his right hand and placed it on her leather armor. The power soon started to flow—not into Zara herself, but into the armor, which began to resonate and glow. "Well, that's interesting. You can put energy into things that didn't have it before. Now, take that energy out and put it directly into me." She moved his hand to one of the few areas of bare skin on her chest.

Tarkas felt nervous but allowed a small amount of power to transfer. "Is it working?"

"Yes, and it feels incredible. Did you have to be my nephew? This is the most amazing feeling I've ever had." She sighed, almost laughing.

Tarkas started to feel uncomfortable and pulled his hand away. "Hey, I'm getting pretty hungry. Can we take a break for food or something?"

She sighed. "Yes, that's all I need from you for today. We'll practice a bit more tomorrow, but if I let you go now, I'll have to put the shackles on you again." Her long nails grazed his wrists.

"Why do I have to be bound when you know I'm staying?" Tarkas asked.

"Are you? Airis might think that, and you may even want that, but I know your friend is out for justice. I paid for you—you're not here of your own free will." She tightened her grasp on his wrist.

He glared back at her. "Why am I really here? Did you think you could just buy me onto your side?"

She stepped back and picked up one of the red, glowing rocks. "Your friends are doomed. I'm giving you the reasons you need to join me and offering you a chance. I assure you, no chief from the Crystal Caves has ever been strong enough to take on the gods. There have been a few over the centuries." She crushed the rock in her hand.

Tarkas thought deeply about what she had said and considered his next move. "What is your end goal, then? What's the plan?"

She sighed. "I'm not a creator god. We had our own stories about the creators and believe we were cursed by our gods. I've been around for over a thousand years, and many of us are just waiting to die. We've done it all and seen it all. Life is fragile and chaotic. We need to end the pain and pettiness—one ruler, one magic. And who would be a better ruler than someone who could live forever?"

"When you say 'one magic,' what about the magic users who live? What if one of them becomes more powerful than you?"

"That's where you come in. Magic normally can't be combined with other types, but there are a few exceptions. I was originally working out how to absorb all magic, so I began hoarding it until I figured out how to absorb it fully. That's what I did with the Crystal Caves. I was just going to kill all the other magic users, but now, with you, I can drain them, and they can live. So you'll be saving lives." She grinned.

Tarkas's mind instantly went to Kaste and the thought of draining him of his powers, imagining something like what happened to Merv happening to the other magic users. He wasn't convinced her intentions were justified. "I see."

"So, do you want to go back to your chains in Airis's room, or should we practice more?" She gestured to the shackles on the ground.

"I'll train more. I'm curious to learn and to practice."

She grinned. "Good." And they returned to the training.

In the evening, Tarkas was returned to Airis's room. Airis kissed Tarkas on the lips as he accepted the transfer from Zara. Airis pulled Tarkas into the room and pinned him to the wall, kissing him.

Tarkas resisted, pushing Airis back. "Slow down, I just got here. What did you do all day? Are we just going to be physical? I'm tired."

Airis frowned. "I missed you and haven't seen you in years. I'm making up for lost time. Does anything else matter?"

Tarkas glared. "I missed you too, but yes, all the other stuff matters if you want a relationship with me."

Airis was taken aback and glared at Tarkas. "You've changed. What's going on?"

"I've changed?" Tarkas replied with a glare. "I'm not a teenager who sees you every day. You faked your death to run off with a sorceress, didn't let me in on your plan, then returned to kill your people and never came to check on me. I don't know you anymore. I didn't see you at my training today, so I want to know what you were doing."

Airis sighed. "You have a good point. I was researching magic for our next planned attack—we're heading to the swamps of Molav to acquire their power. Plock, Kellwyn, and I went over the landscape, and another of our team, Malwick, who you haven't met yet, is scouting the political structure of the area. We have scouts all over the place. Are you satisfied?"

"It's a start," Tarkas answered.

"Good," Airis said, leaning in to kiss Tarkas again, only to be blocked once more. "What now?"

"I told you I was tired and not in the mood. Does our relationship have to just be about sex?" Tarkas asked.

Airis glared. "Tarkas, I've missed you. I want to be close to you."

Tarkas held up his shackled wrists. "You're in charge of my freedom, and we were intimate—what more do you want?"

"I know this, but it still feels like you're resisting me. Why? You're here to be with me, so why aren't you doing what I ask?"

"Because I'm my own person with my own needs. Sex isn't everything in a relationship. I need rest, and then we can talk about doing things," Tarkas explained.

Airis paused. "You've just never said no to me before." He thought for a moment. "Fine, have your rest. When you're done, I'll ask again."

Tarkas sighed, not the answer he had hoped for, but it was a compromise that would do for now. At least Airis would leave him alone for a while. "Thank you." He raised his hands. "Are you going to remove these shackles and lock the door like last night?"

Airis paused for a moment, then stepped toward the door. "No, you don't need your hands." He opened the door, stepped out, and cast a spell to lock Tarkas in.

Tarkas was resting on the bed when he was awoken in the night by the door opening. Tarkas sat up in bed, surprised to see it wasn't Airis but the elf mage. "Kellwyn, is that you?" Tarkas asked. "What are you doing here?"

"I assume Kaley must have told you my name. I'm here to talk to you about what's going on with you and Airis. He left this room upset hours ago, and well, if you're going to be staying, we need to work this out." He entered the room and closed the door behind him.

"Then why isn't he here to talk to me about this?" Tarkas asked.

"Because he doesn't want to hurt you and isn't thinking clearly right now. So I'm here to analyze the situation." He moved closer, standing in front of Tarkas sternly. "You're here, no matter what, whether you get along with Airis or not. Zara just thought you two would enjoy each other and it would motivate you to stay."

Tarkas let out a deep sigh. "My issue isn't with being with Airis. If I'm going to be here longer, I don't want our entire relationship to be about sex. I know Zara bought me, but I need to know—am I here as a slave or as part of the team?"

Kellwyn considered this for a moment. "I see the issue. Well, the plan was that you would eventually join us once we could trust you and knew you were committed. But you'll remain in Airis's care until that day, and whatever he chooses to do with you is his choice. If you two can't work things out, you can be placed in my care—and it won't be as pleasant. So I suggest you find a way to work things out."

"I would if he would come in here and talk to me," Tarkas said. "A lot has changed since I last saw him, and he thinks we're still the same. I'm willing to make it work if he'll listen."

Kellwyn leaned in closer and blew softly on Tarkas's face, making Tarkas's lips glow. "I don't believe you. Who is the other lover?"

Tarkas glared. "What are you talking about?"

"Someone put a tracking spell on your lips. Who kissed you?"

Tarkas's eyes widened, and without realizing it, he muttered. "Kaste."

"Kaste, as in Plock's brother? Interesting," Kellwyn replied.

Tarkas stood up and shook his bound hands. "Look, it's not what you think. I didn't know he did that. I'm not resisting because of him."

Kellwyn waved his hand over Tarkas's side and detected another tracking spell on his armor. "Doesn't matter why. Your friends might be planning an attack, but they won't survive. Get used to your new home." He then wiped his hand over the two tracking spells, removing them.

"What did you do?" Tarkas asked.

"Sent your friends a message. Now they know we're aware." Kellwyn turned to leave the room. "I'll send Airis in."

"Is he outside? Because I'd like to ask you some questions," Tarkas said.

Kellwyn turned back, staring blankly at Tarkas. "No, Airis is drinking in the kitchen. What would you like to ask?"

"I want to know why you joined Zara. You were a temple mage, right? Protecting your people's most sacred item—why hand it over to her?" Tarkas asked.

"Just because I was a temple mage doesn't mean I liked the job. All the elven mages end up there eventually. Elven culture is strict—if you're born into a role, that's your destiny, no choice. I could have left, but after the war, it was unwise to leave the city. Zara offered me a way out and a better job. I don't mind being a mage, but I want it on my own terms, not because the queen assigned it. I helped Zara take the gem because I wanted to teach the queen a lesson."

"I see," Tarkas replied.

"Zara isn't that bad of a leader. I prefer her over Keltrice. Since the war with King Alaric, Keltrice has worsened—locked the gates and kept the elves contained. I was a child at the time, so I saw the change. I prefer Zara's plans." He paused. "Does that answer your question?"

Tarkas nodded. "Yeah, it does. You can bring Airis in now. I'm ready to talk to him. Please don't mention Kaste."

Kellwyn turned to the door, then glanced back at Tarkas one last time before leaving. "I encourage you to work things out with him, because in my care, it won't be as pleasurable."

Tarkas sat on the bed for a few moments, looking at the small stone room. Beside the bed was a stone table, with no windows. In the corner were Airis's staff and skull mask.

Moments later, Airis entered the room. "I'm sorry for the way I acted earlier. There's just a lot going on."

Tarkas smiled. "Airis, I know there is. I have a lot of conflicting emotions right now. I just need to know—do you want me as a lover or a slave?"

Airis glared. "Why would I want you as a slave? I just want us to go back to the way things were. Sure, this isn't my family yurt, but it's cozy, and there's lots of travel. Let's work together." He moved closer to kiss Tarkas.

"That's what I'm talking about," Tarkas said, leaning back. "You tell me something I want to hear, and then, without waiting for my response, you make a move. I haven't given you an answer yet."

Airis held up his hands and stepped back. "All right, I get it. I'll back off. Please, speak."

Tarkas took a deep breath. "It's a nice offer, and yes, I think with time we can get back to a loving relationship, but it's not going to happen overnight."

Airis scowled. "You're not going back to your other friends, so why is it going to take time?"

Tarkas raised an eyebrow. "I need time to grieve and adjust. Why are you so needy?"

Airis sighed. "I asked you before if you moved on after I left, and you said no. But is there someone else?"

Tarkas glared. "I told you I need time to adjust; that isn't a rejection. If you missed me so much, why didn't you come back? You asked if I was with anyone in the tribe. I have been with others, but nothing serious." Tarkas paused. "Is that what this is about? You're jealous and haven't been with anyone else in the last five years?"

Airis's eyes flashed red. "I couldn't go back, and I didn't know we'd kill everyone. Yes, I'm jealous—you were committed to me."

Tarkas groaned. "You were dead as far as anyone knew. I wasn't going to wait for your resurrection."

Airis took a deep breath, clenching his fists at his sides. "Fair, but I'm here now, and no one else matters."

Tarkas was unsure of what was going on in Airis's mind, but he stood up and moved closer. "You're right—no one else does. Let's keep it that way." He leaned in to kiss Airis.

Airis took a breath, calmed down, and kissed Tarkas back. "You're right. You're here, and you're mine." He grabbed Tarkas's shoulders and pushed him against the wall, continuing to kiss him.

Tarkas struggled to move his arms. "Can you take these shackles off so I can use my arms?"

While kissing Tarkas's face and neck, Airis reached into his pocket and fiddled with the shackles, unlocking them. Tarkas embraced Airis, and they soon began to take off their armor before moving to the bed. Tarkas felt less involved and focused than before; he was giving in because he knew his rescue party was due sometime today, and Airis was not thinking clearly. While on the bed, Tarkas felt a burning pinch on the back of his neck, making him twitch, but it wasn't painful enough to stop. Once they were done, they lay in bed with Airis keeping an arm draped over Tarkas.

Tarkas ran his hands through Airis's hair. "Hey, Airis, are you starting to go bald?"

Airis lifted his head. "Yeah, dark magic will do that to you. Every time I use it, it's a small price to pay. I'm glad your wounds are healing."

Tarkas looked at one of the necrotic wounds on his upper arm and noticed that it had improved. "Huh, you're right. I didn't notice that before. I guess they'll heal with time."

"Yeah, that's nice. I liked your lovely skin," Airis said, running his hands over Tarkas's bare chest.

They lay in an embrace until there was a knock at the door, and then the lock was opened by magic. "Are you two done? I need your boyfriend, Tarkas, for a bit," Zara said as she opened the door.

Airis sat up and frowned at her. "Why do you need him?"

"It's the middle of the day, and I need him. You'll be needed soon, so get ready," Zara said, standing firm in the room.

Airis got out of bed and started dressing. Tarkas was still lying down. "Ugh, are you going to leave the room, or at least turn your head?"

"No, I need to make sure you two do as I say. Get dressed," she said, devoid of emotion.

Tarkas got out of bed and began putting on his armor, then followed Zara out of the room. She was silent as she led him up a set of stone stairs to an opening in the mountains. In the distance, Tarkas could see his rescue party.

"Did your friends really think they could plan a surprise attack on me?" Zara said, looking at the small army on the horizon.

Tarkas's heart dropped. "How long have you known?"

"Since I picked you up. I knew they would come for you, and I knew you were planning an attack, but I thought maybe I could convince you to stay."

Tarkas glared at her. "You didn't talk to me; you bought me, then expected me to side with you after keeping me locked up and previously having me tortured?"

She turned to him, placing her hand on his bearded face. "Dear Tarkas, I need you for the next step in my plan, whether you like it or not. I gave you time with your lover and, hopefully, a new sense of family. I know it might be a shock, but in time, I think you'll come to accept this new family."

Their eyes locked, and in an instant, he saw deep into her soul—a thousand years of pain. He realized she wasn't doing this out of greed or power but as a way to start over. If she couldn't die, she was going to recreate the world. "What are you going to do?"

She turned away and held up her hand, creating a glowing ball of light in her palm. "Stop them. They're not coming here." She prepared to throw the ball of magic at the approaching army, but Tarkas lunged at her, knocking her down and sending the ball into the mountains instead.

"No more killing!" he shouted.

She snarled at him. "Whose side are you on?!"

"I'm on the side of peace. I lost my entire family and culture because of your killing. This isn't because of time—it's because people like you feel they can rule the world. No more killing. Merv gave you what you wanted, and you killed him. He was on your side—how can I or anyone else trust you?"

She stood up, this time her magic ball pointed at him. He drew his bow. "Don't do it."

She threw the ball, which quickly hit his bow, charging it with power. Tarkas paused to examine the bow as her eyes widened. He raised the bow again, aiming it at her. Suddenly, there was a rumble in the mountain. Both Tarkas and Zara lost their balance.

"Is this mountain a volcano?" Tarkas asked.

She shook her head. "No, your friends are here." She tried to run for the trapdoor back into the mountain, but Tarkas blocked her and kicked her, knocking her down. "You're not getting away from this so easily." He aimed his bow at her again.

Another shake struck, and both of them fell down the side of the mountain, rolling for what felt like forever, hitting trees along the way. Tarkas did his best to curl into a ball to protect himself. Eventually, he landed with a heavy thunk, his head still spinning. Skolsav saw him and hurried over. "That was quite a fall. Are you okay?"

Tarkas rubbed his head. "Where is everyone? Zara—she fell too. Go find her. My arm hurts, but find Zara."

Skolsav stood up and looked around. "I didn't see her, but some of us went ahead. The army will be here soon." He helped Tarkas sit up. "You need medical attention. I'll call over someone to look at you and go search for Zara." He let out a loud whistle, and soon a soldier came running over to check on Tarkas.

The soldier examined Tarkas's wounds. "Don't move; you're badly hurt."

"Zara fell down with me. Find her. And where's my bow? Where's Dorak?" Tarkas said faintly, struggling to stay conscious.

"We'll find her and take care of everything." The soldier turned to Skolsav. "Go get one of the mages; he needs their help."

Skolsav stood up. "I'll get Kaste. I'll be right back."

Tarkas tried to stay conscious but soon passed out before he could say anything else.

Dorak and the Rescue of Tarkas

Dorak crashed through the mountain doors, smashing them as he went.

"I told you to be quiet when we entered," Kaste said.

"Doesn't matter—we're here now." Dorak drew his axe. "Where is Tarkas?!" he shouted.

The elf mage, Kellwyn, stepped forward. "Get out now!"

Dorak threw his axe at the mage. "Don't tell me what to do!"

The mage stopped the axe mid-air, attempting to control it. Kaste sent a fireball toward him. "Listen to him, or things will get worse for you."

Kellwyn turned his attention to Kaste, dropping the axe and sending a magic spike at him. Kaste deflected it, and they engaged in battle with each other.

Dorak continued further in, followed by Kal and Lira, as they moved deeper into the mine. They split up to cover more ground. Prince Veylin followed Dorak. Soon, they encountered Plock. Upon seeing Dorak with his axe, Plock put up a magic shield. "Don't hurt me! I'm just banging Zara. I surrender!"

Dorak reached around the simple mage shield and glared at him. "Where are Zara and Tarkas?"

Plock lowered the shield and pointed down the hall. "Over there, you'll find a set of stairs. They went up today. Don't kill me."

Dorak grunted and dragged Plock back toward the entrance, calling out. "Kaste, I found your brother. He's as fearful as you." He tossed Plock in the direction they had come from.

Prince Veylin spoke up. "We need to capture these people and have them face justice."

Dorak turned to glare at him. "Plock wasn't there the day our people were killed. He has nothing to do with me—Kaste wants him, he can deal with his brother. Now don't get in my way." Dorak went further into the cave as the others broke off to check the outer rooms. Dorak was focused solely on finding his friend and stopping Zara. He banged on the cave walls to announce his approach. Soon, he found the stairs and began climbing. Prince Veylin followed close behind.

"Be careful. I don't think the mine was made to hold this many people—it's rumbling," Prince Veylin warned.

Dorak turned and grunted. "Don't get in the way. I know caves, and this one is fine!" He continued up the stairs, the prince still behind him. The mountain shook a little more. At the top of the stairs, Dorak saw Tarkas and Zara stumbling as the mountain rumbled. Dorak rushed to catch them before they fell, reaching out to grab whoever he could. He looked up and realized he had grabbed Zara's leg. His first thought was to drop her, but then he considered whether Tarkas could survive the fall. He pulled Zara toward him. "I have you now!"

She lifted her hand to shoot an energy beam at him. "Not so fast, barbarian!"

He held onto her ankle with one hand and drew his axe with the other. "I think you'll find that I have the upper hand. As chief of the protectors of the Crystal Caves, you must comply with the punishment that is to befall you!"

She threw the energy ball at Dorak, but he blocked it with his battle axe, which absorbed the energy. Fear filled her eyes as he raised the axe toward her. Prince Veylin grabbed the axe handle, stopping it just a foot from Zara. "I told you, you're in the kingdom of Alwyndia. You cannot enforce your people's punishments here—she must face judgment."

Dorak turned and snarled at him. "All this pain and suffering could end right now, and you want to throw that away for laws and procedure?"

"Yes, barbarian," Prince Veylin said firmly.

Zara sent another energy ball at the two of them. Prince Veylin shifted Dorak's axe, blocking the attack, and the axe absorbed the energy once more. The prince removed his belt and took out a set of shackles Kaste had given him on the road. These shackles were warded to prevent the wearer from using magic. "No more energy blasts from you. You're coming with us to face trial." He fastened the shackles on Zara.

She let out a loud cackle. "I knew your great-great-grandfather when he wrote the laws of your kingdom after he took it from King Varis. I have seen your empire rise and fall. Your laws can't do anything to me—they're flawed constructs to make you feel powerful and give you a false sense of security. Do what you will."

"So, are you coming willingly?" Prince Veylin asked.

"Yes, take me where you must," she said, raising her shackled hands.

Dorak grunted. "I don't trust her." The mountain rumbled again.

"Come on, we don't have much time; the mountain is collapsing," Prince Veylin said, gripping Zara's shackles and heading back to the stairs. "I'm not sure it's safe to go back down."

Dorak took the first steps down the stairs. "Don't be a coward. The mine isn't going to collapse—it's just settling with all the people inside. So come on, unless you have a better way."

They followed Dorak down the stairs and turned toward the corridor leading to the entrance. There, they saw Kaste and Plock fighting. Plock turned his attention from his brother to Dorak and Zara. He focused an energy beam on Dorak. "Let Mistress Zara go!"

Dorak blocked it with his axe, absorbing the attack. "Don't fire at me again, or you will feel the blade of my axe. You are not the one I have issue with, so go back to your brother."

Plock glared getting ready to shoot another energy ball. "Zara is my lover you will not hurt her!"

Dorak ran up and pinned Plock against the wall, holding the axe to his throat. "What did I say? I'll chop your head off right now, but you're not my enemy, so back off."

Plock put his hands down. "Alright, just don't hurt her."

Dorak glared at him. "Don't tell me what to do when it isn't your family."

The cave became unstable and started shaking more. Dorak pulled back his axe and stepped away. "There are too many people in this cave. We've got to get out—it's unstable!"

Plock ran toward the cave's opening. Dorak followed, with Zara and Prince Veylin close behind. As they made their way out, the cave continued to rumble. Once outside, they saw one of the other mages restraining Kellwyn.

"Get out of the way!" Dorak grabbed Plock's collar and shouted. "Where is Kaste? I have his brother!"

Skolsav rushed over. "He's with Tarkas. Tarkas is hurt."

Dorak dragged Plock as he rushed to Tarkas's side, following Skolsav. Kaste had his hands over Tarkas, trying to heal him while Tarkas lay unconscious.

"Kaste, get out of the way and take your brother."

"I'm trying to heal Tarkas. It doesn't seem to be working," Kaste replied.

"He's a conduit. He doesn't heal the same way. I know how, so take your brother," Dorak demanded.

They switched places. Dorak took the canteen of water from his belt and knelt beside Tarkas. "Hold onto your brother this time." He placed the canteen to Tarkas's lips. A moment later, Tarkas woke up, coughing.

Kaste, now standing with Plock by his side, spoke up. "What kind of magic was that?"

"Yeah, how does water just revive someone?" Plock added.

"It isn't just any water. It's from the Fountain of Life. It saved him once before, and I was given more for a case like this," Dorak explained.

Tarkas sat up and took a deep breath. "Yeah, that felt good. Where is Zara? And my bow? We fell off the mountain together."

Dorak grunted. "Zara's been captured by Prince Veylin, and we'll go look for your bow."

Tarkas stood up. "So, what now?"

"If I had it my way, they'd all be dead already. But we're heading back soon," Dorak said.

Tarkas looked around at the people gathered nearby. "Where is Airis? Has anyone seen him?"

Dorak's eyes filled with rage. He had been so focused on Zara that Airis had slipped his mind. "No. Where is that asshole?"

The cave started rumbling again. "Too many people around! This mine isn't stable!" Dorak called out.

A look of worry crossed Tarkas's face. "Is everyone out of the cave?"

"How many were there?" Dorak asked.

Tarkas paused to think. "Four plus myself. I didn't see anyone else."

"Well, I think everyone's out, but I haven't seen Airis. He might've gone out the back way," Plock said.

Kaste frowned. "There's a back exit?"

Plock grinned. "There are a lot of things about this mine you don't know."

Dorak roared. "We don't have time for this—it could collapse!" He rushed to get everyone away from the cave.

Tarkas began climbing up the mountain. "I'm going to find my bow."

"But the side of the mountain isn't stable!" Kaste called after him.

"I have to find it!" Tarkas replied. "I know caves. I'll be safe."

He climbed up the side of the mountain, searching for his bow, a striking piece of saturated red petrified wood. As he climbed through the thicket of trees, he spotted blood and torn bits of his clothing on branches, along with a few arrows scattered on the ground. He pressed on, nearing the top but still hidden among the trees. Finally, he saw his bow.

As Tarkas reached for it, he noticed the hand holding the bow.

"Airis, please give me my bow," Tarkas requested.

Airis held up the bow with a sinister grin. "Why? So you can shoot me with it? Or because you're weak without it—only good at archery and never skilled in combat?"

"Airis, you know that isn't true. It's my bow. That's why I want it back. I won't hurt you," Tarkas said calmly.

"You won't hurt me? You've already hurt me," Airis said.

Tarkas sighed. "Airis, listen. That bow is very important to me—now give it back."

Airis toyed with the bow in his hand.

"Airis, you died and left me. It's been five years. I've changed since then, and so have you. You're not the same man I knew back when we were teens, planning to move into your mother's yurt. You're not the man I would spend my patrols of the caves with. Where is that man? The one who came to me the night your father died, unsure of how you could be a good hunter to take care of your mother because you were a magic user. Where is my Airis?"

Airis gripped the bow tightly, his eyes beginning to glow red. "You're right—that Airis is gone. That Airis died because of Gorak's rules. You thought it was hard growing up not as strong as everyone else? At least you could try! I was barred from so many things. Faking my death was the best thing I ever did, and I regret none of it!"

Tarkas, knowing he had struck a nerve, wasted no time. He lunged forward to grab the bow, but Airis pulled it back. Tarkas caught hold of Airis's hand holding the bow.

"And don't regret this," Tarkas said as he began to drain the magic from Airis. He watched as the power drained from Airis's glowing eyes, and the hand holding the bow began to wither.

Airis looked down at his arm, watching it age and mummify before he jerked it away, dropping the bow. "By the gods, what have you done to me?"

"I asked you to give me my bow," Tarkas said, picking up the bow.

Airis glared at Tarkas and attempted to form an energy ball, but nothing happened. "What did you do to me?"

Tarkas nocked an arrow and aimed his bow at Airis. "I drained some of your magic. Now come with me—you're being taken into custody along with the rest of our friends."

"No. You think you can stop me?" Airis grinned. "I know you better than you know yourself. I know you won't shoot me because part of you still hopes I'll return to the man you once knew. And you think taking my magic will somehow help me along the way."

Tarkas drew his bow further. "I've died too, Airis. In that time, I've also changed. I'm not the same man you knew. Now, come with me, or I will shoot."

"You'll have to shoot me before I ever surrender—"

"Then take a hit from my axe!" Dorak yelled, charging forward with his axe raised.

Airis summoned a burst of magic to create a shield, blocking the blow. "Oh, Dorak. We meet again. And you think you can stop me?"

Dorak pressed his axe against the force field. "I know you're weak, and I have no problem cutting off your head!"

Airis grinned and released the shield, ducking as Dorak's axe sliced his sleeve. He snapped his fingers and vanished.

Dorak swung his axe through empty air. "Where did he go?"

Tarkas lowered his bow. "I think he's gone."

"Aaaaaaaahhhhhh!" Dorak let out a furious scream. "Tarkas, next time you have the chance to shoot—shoot!"

Tarkas put his bow away. "I'm sorry. I didn't expect to see him."

Dorak clenched his fists and grunted. "I can't be mad at you, but next time, let me deal with Airis, okay?"

"I just went to find my bow. I didn't know he had it," Tarkas said, pausing. Somehow, he felt Dorak understood. "I think that would be best. Can we go now?"

Dorak placed a hand on Tarkas's shoulder. "Yeah, let's head back."

They climbed down the mountain, rejoined the party, and made their way back to Alwyndia to confront their enemies.

Dorak and the Trial of Zara

Three days had passed since they returned, and Tarkas lay in his bed. After everything that had happened, he decided it was best to stay at the Mages' College. He hadn't spoken much in those days, choosing to be reclusive, reflecting on the events—and on his loss of Airis. He lay there, his mind looping over everything that had transpired.

There was a knock at the door.

"Hey, it's Kaste. I was wondering if you'd like to talk?"

"I'm not really in the mood for anything, Kaste," Tarkas paused. "But... you can come in."

Kaste entered the room. "How are you really doing after everything?"

Tarkas sighed. "Not well. It was pretty traumatic, and I don't know what to do after all of it. How is your brother doing?"

Kaste sighed. "My brother is rotting in a cell right now while they figure out what to do with him. I have to go back later today and advocate for his release into my custody."

"I'm glad you got your brother back. I think I've lost more this time," Tarkas said, sitting up in his bed. He sighed again. "Kaste, I don't think, after everything I've learned, that I can continue a relationship with you."

Kaste let out a sigh of relief. "Phew. I was trying to figure out how to break it off with you. No offense—I like you—but once you left, I realized I got this amazing power boost from you, and that's probably what attracted me in the first place. I didn't want to build anything on that. Also, if I get my brother back, I'll be focusing on him, probably moving back home."

"I want a break from magic for now. It's caused me nothing but pain. I think Airis got the same boost you did—but he's addicted to it," Tarkas said, rubbing the back of his neck.

"Can I sit next to you?" Kaste asked, craning his neck to look.

"Oh, yeah—sit down." Tarkas patted the space on the bed next to him.

Kaste took the seat and examined the back of Tarkas's neck. "What exactly happened to you in those three days?"

Tarkas narrowed his eyes at him. "A bunch of things—but I know you're asking because you noticed something. What is it?"

"Hold still." Kaste pulled aside Tarkas's collar and stiffened when he saw what was there. "You're not going to like this, but you need to tell me exactly what happened—right now."

"How bad is it?" Tarkas asked, his heart racing with worry. "Zara told me about my parents and taught me how to use my abilities, and then Airis tried to make me his slave. I didn't tell him about you, but he figured it out. What is it?"

Kaste took a deep breath. "I'm going to assume Airis did this. Someone put a branding spell on you."

Tarkas shot a glare at him. "Tell me it's not as bad as it sounds! And how do I get rid of it?"

"There's no way to remove it—because it was placed using dark magic. The caster has to give something up for the spell to work. Have you noticed anything different about Airis?"

Tarkas clenched his fists. "Yeah, he's balding, but that asshole had the nerve to brand me! I thought he just bit me. What does this do, and how do we fix it?"

"Okay, let me think. I haven't seen something like this in years." Kaste pondered, twiddling his fingers. "The spell is sort of a tracker, but it takes a lot of energy to maintain. It means you're bound to the user who placed it. Maybe, since you're a conduit, you can remove its power—but it's strong."

"Can't we just burn it off or cut it out? It's only skin-deep, right?" Tarkas rubbed the spot, trying to feel it.

"Like I said, it's dark magic—not so easy. You can't burn these off." Kaste took Tarkas's hand and guided it to the spot. "Draining its magic is the best option we have."

Tarkas let out a sigh. "I hate magic." He closed his eyes, focusing on removing the magic. His hand twitched as he held it, his teeth gritting and face contorting in pain. After a moment, he stopped. "I think I got it. That was terrible. You're right—dark magic is different."

Kaste took a coin out of his pocket and pressed it against the brand. "Yeah, it seems to be drained of magic. So, you have a scar, and let's hope the magic doesn't return. This is beyond my expertise now. I should really write this down—conduits are so rare, I could write the book on this."

Tarkas laughed. "Go ahead. Someone needs to. For me, it'll just be about getting past this now. I have no idea what I'm supposed to do. It's like when I came back to life—I returned to a completely different world. Now I don't know how to adjust. It's like I went to bed and woke up with a whole new family, no home, and a world where everything and everyone is different."

Kaste placed his hand on Tarkas's shoulder. "I'm sorry. This must really be hard for you."

"When this all started, it felt like me and Dorak were just going on another adventure—like a hunting party or something. It was that night, when we found their camp, that I realized I couldn't go back. Things were never going to be the same." Tarkas let out a long sigh. "I just don't know what this all means for me going forward."

"Wow, that's rough. I don't know what I can do, but just know I'm someone you can talk to about this. I'm not going to pressure you into anything," Kaste said.

"Thanks. That's one thing I'm really enjoying on this journey—the new friends I'm making. It's nice to meet people I haven't known my whole life. I didn't realize the world is so big," Tarkas said.

"It's much bigger. I haven't been everywhere, but I've heard of a few places. Maybe when this whole mess is over, we can explore the rest of the world."

"Oh, and when you talk to your brother, ask him about the other members. Airis mentioned to me that they had others. If you could find out who and where they are, that would help. I know Dorak's only going to be worried about Airis and Zara's fate, but I feel like the others might want to continue her—or their—work."

Kaste paused to absorb the information. "I'll find out what my brother knows."

"I want to talk to my brother first!" Kaste said, arguing with the guards at the palace prison.

"Now, sir, I cannot let you speak to him before the hearing. He is a magic user, and they are not allowed to talk to anyone beforehand," the guard told him.

"Look, I'm a magic user too—and he is my twin. If anyone is most protected from him, it's me," Kaste tried to convince the guards.

"Sorry, but the only one who can give you permission is the queen," the guards said. "But the hearing is not far off now."

Kaste, feeling defeated, paused for a moment—when Prince Veylin showed up.

"Veylin, please tell them that I need to talk to my brother," Kaste said.

Prince Veylin narrowed his eyes toward Kaste. "Why do you need to talk to him? I came down here to retrieve Zara for her hearing."

"I need to talk to him and find out what he knows before he's punished. He's my twin, and I need him. If I can speak to him, I might be able to get more information," Kaste pleaded.

Prince Joren thought about it for a moment. "I don't have much time to think this over, but I'll allow it—and you'd better make progress and not just conspire with him." He turned to the guard. "Captain Reyne, could you let Kaste in to talk to his brother, and then come help me with transporting Zara?"

Captain Reyne nodded. "Right away, Your Highness." He took the keys from his belt and turned to Kaste. "Follow me."

He led Kaste down the hall to Plock's cell and opened the door. "He's in there. Do you mind if I leave you for a bit?"

"His trial is right after Zara's, so I don't mind staying here with him. Thank you."

Kaste entered the cell, which was locked behind him. From the hallway, he could hear Solmack talking to another guard, instructing them to keep watch—and to note that one of them wasn't a prisoner.

Kaste turned to Plock, who was sitting in the corner of the cell on a small wooden bench that may have also served as his bed. Kaste went over and sat down next to his brother.

"Hey. How are you doing?"

"What am I doing here? All I did was fall in love," Plock said.

"You fell in love with a woman who was bent on taking over the world. It wasn't just the person. But hey—we can go back to the way things were before," Kaste said.

"I don't want things to go back to the way they were. I want to be with her. I really liked her, and I think she would be great for the family. You should join us," Plock said.

Kaste narrowed his eyes, suspecting there was a chance Zara had enchanted Plock and he was still under her influence. "Alright, I'll hear you out. What's so great about her? And how does the operation run?"

"Mistress Zara, you stand accused of crimes of genocide, theft, destruction of property, and acts of violence against multiple kingdoms. Representatives from those kingdoms are here today to decide your fate," Queen Navessa said. "Do you have anything to say for yourself?"

Zara stood in the center of a simple wooden room—almost like a barn—the least elegant building in the entire kingdom. Seated before her were Dorak, Queen Navessa, Prince Veylin, Prince Kal, Lira, and Master Dormir. Guards lined the walls of the building.

Zara scoffed. "My reasons are my own, but I admit to all the crimes. Do your worst," she said with an arrogant smile.

Queen Navessa stared down at her. "I myself don't have charges to bring, but I am allied with these other kingdoms. So, I am at liberty to hand you over to them—unless you can give me a good reason not to."

"I seek to start a new world order. If you're willing to sign your kingdom over to me, then sure—hand me over to whoever you feel you must," Zara said coldly.

Queen Navessa turned to Lira. "Since your kingdom is the closest, I'm asking you—what do you want done with Zara?"

"She stole a valuable magical artifact from us, which was thankfully recovered in the raid. However, she and her crew also damaged one of our temples. She needs to be taken back to our kingdom and held before our queen. If she can show some remorse as we return the artifact, that may help her case," Lira explained.

"Alright," Queen Navessa said, turning to Kal and Dorak. "Prince Kal and Chief Dorak—what does your kingdom propose?"

Kal spoke first. "Oh, I'm not a prince anymore—it's just Kal now. I only know the laws of my father, King Alaric. She didn't attack our kingdom directly, but the Crystal Caves have their own governing laws, so I defer to Dorak."

Dorak grunted. "Death. She committed the worst and most horrendous of atrocities against my people—genocide. She must be put to death. Any place will do. I can do it right here." He lifted his battle axe.

Queen Navessa raised her hands. "Please—no killing in the justice hall. We are here to decide her fate."

She turned back to Lira. "Is death the punishment she would face in your kingdom?"

"That's not my place to say. It's one possible punishment, but I cannot say for certain," Lira responded.

Dorak spoke up again. "You can take the others back to your queen. When my village was attacked, Zara and Airis were the only two there. You can have Kaste and Plock—I want Zara."

Kaley paused for a moment and thought. "I would prefer to take all of them to Queen Keltrice. But I think we have an issue—her magic. We'll need to suppress it for transport." She turned her attention to Master Dormir. "Is there a magic spell to suppress her abilities?"

Master Dormir spoke up. "Technically, yes—but I do not know if it will work at her level—"

"That's why we should kill her now," Dorak interjected. "She may attack us on our way to Kelonia, and you could bring your queen the head of her enemy!"

"I'm not opposed to that idea," Master Dormir added. "But you also have Tarkas—maybe he can remove her magic so that she can be transported."

Dorak grunted. "He doesn't have magic! And he wouldn't do it. But with my axe, I can subdue her and keep her in line."

Everyone who wasn't Dorak looked around at each other. Kal spoke up. "I will take it as my responsibility—to watch and make sure that Zara gets to Kelonia alive. I trust Dorak will respect the laws of other nations."

Dorak gave a disgruntled sigh. "Yes, I will respect them. But I'll say this—the longer she stays alive, the more danger you put everyone in."

Lira spoke up. "Then if she causes any issues on the journey, I will give you the right to subdue her—but not to abuse that power."

"I can agree to that," Dorak grunted.

"In that case," Queen Navessa said. "I will release Zara into your custody, Lira, and she will remain in the prison until you choose to depart. Is this agreed?"

Everyone nodded.

"Alright. Man-at-arms, please take her back to her cell and bring out Kellwyn and Plock."

There was a short recess while the guards exchanged the prisoners. Master Dormir entered the room and switched seats with Dorak.

"Master Dormir, why are you here? And Dorak—where are you going?" Prince Joren asked.

"These two didn't attack my people. I don't care about their fate," Dorak said and went to the back of the room, taking a seat.

Master Dormir leaned toward the prince. "Plock is my student and a member of the College of Magic. His punishment falls under my jurisdiction."

The queen spoke up. "Does anyone else have reason to judge Plock and Kellwyn?"

Kal spoke up. "Just to clarify—Plock and Kellwyn didn't attack the Crystal Caves, but they did align themselves with Zara, and I would like to have a say."

The queen nodded. "Agreed. You may remain."

Soon after, Kellwyn and Plock were brought out by the guards and seated. Kaste sat beside his brother. The queen looked at him.

"You don't have to sit next to your brother. You can sit up here with us."

"I prefer to sit beside him as counsel, not as his judge," Kaste replied.

"Alright then. Let's get this started," the queen said. "Kellwyn and Plock—you both stand accused of stealing a sacred artifact, destruction of property, and assisting in treasonous activities."

"And for Plock—breaking your oath to the College of Magic," Master Dormir added.

"Yes, that too," the queen acknowledged. "So, what do you have to say for yourselves?"

Kellwyn spoke up. "My comments will be shared with my queen, Keltrice, and not with you. My involvement in this is purely political."

Kaley spoke up. "Then in that case, you will share them with me. I am here to determine whether you should be brought back to Queen Keltrice."

Kellwyn said. "Fine. If you must know—I'm against the choices that Queen Keltrice has made since the war, and I remain loyal to the usurper King Marion. Closing the gates to the city was wrong. She needs less power, not more."

"I thought we ended the movement of Marion. How are you still around?" Kaley asked.

"I'm a magic user—we live longer. And there are many of us still around. I'm more open about my alignment because, as a magic user, I can't be removed. We can no longer leave the city to grow our skills or trade, so I'll say what I want about the queen. I met Zara a long time ago and only used magic to contact her again recently."

"How recently?" Kal asked.

Kellwyn was caught off guard by the question. "I'd have to think—about ten years ago, we started corresponding again. And if you're wondering, the attacks have been well-planned."

Queen Navessa looked at everyone. "Well, in that case—does anyone have a judgment for Kellwyn?"

Kaley spoke up. "Yes. He will be returned to Kelownia and face trial and execution there. Members of the Valrick Rebellion were sentenced to death years ago."

"I will accompany you," Master Dormir added. "If there is a group of underground mages, I must assess the situation."

"Alright then. If no one else has anything to add, we'll move on to Plock," Queen Navessa said.

Kaste spoke up. "May I speak for my brother first?"

"If you wish, but you will be responsible for all of his crimes as well—if you are wrong," the queen stated.

Kaste paused for a moment before speaking. "If that is how it must be, then I will accept my fate—because I know that I am right."

"Alright then, say your piece."

"My brother is innocent, and Master Dormir can back this up. My brother was under a charm spell—Zara bewitched him, so he had to follow her will. Now that he is more than 200 feet away from her, the spell has no effect. He needs to be kept away from her. I suggest that he be kept under watch at the Mages' College."

Queen Navessa stared at Plock. "Is what your brother says true?"

Plock took a deep breath. "Yes. I was charmed by Mistress Zara. She came and found me with a group of other mages and invited us to a party—it was wonderful. She gave us food and drink, taught us some new magic tricks, and then she seduced me. After that, I don't remember much. I didn't steal any magical artifacts myself—I was there as her lover. When she needed an extra mage, I helped, but I don't know what my full purpose was to her. I may have been there, but it wasn't of my own free will."

Kaley narrowed her eyes at Plock. "When we last met, your brother wanted to talk to you, and you refused. What was your reason then? You were at the attack on the temple—what do you have to say for yourself?"

"I was bewitched. At the temple, I don't remember much besides just being there. And as for my brother, I knew Zara said I could talk to him, but at the time, I didn't want him to try and convince me to leave the woman I thought I was in love with," Plock said.

Kaley turned to Master Dormir. "How does this charm spell work, and is this believable?"

Master Dormir took a deep breath. "Short answer—yes. The charm spell is very controlling and is a type of dark magic. I wouldn't put it past Zara to use dark magic. Plock is a good and serious mage. He got into some trouble when he was younger, but when he was separated from his brother, he was a very dedicated student. Running off with Zara was completely out of character—that's something his brother Kaste would do."

Kaste shot Master Dormir a glare.

Queen Navessa paused for a moment. "Alright. Is there a way to prove this? Something other than just word of mouth?"

Kaste spoke up. "Yes. We can check him for her magical signature and observe whether his behavior changes when he's within 200 feet of her—but that's risky. She could control him again and make him do something else. I think it's best to keep him far away from her."

"That is true. I think it's best we confine Plock to the Mages' College until this situation is resolved—and we can restrict his use of magic," Master Dormir suggested.

"Is this acceptable to everyone?" the queen asked.

Kaley raised her hand. "No—I need to bring in all those responsible for the attack."

"Kaley, he didn't know. He was being mind-controlled and wasn't aware of what was happening. You already got the two who plotted the attack," Kaste said.

Kaley paused for a long moment before making her decision. "If you can promise that Plock will not enter the city of Kelownia, then I will turn a blind eye to his involvement."

Kaste let out a huge sigh. "Thank you so much for this."

"Don't mention it," Kaley replied.

The queen looked around. "Well then, if that is all, court is dismissed." She rose from her chair and headed out of the room as the guards took Kellwyn away. Kaste was about to leave with his brother when Kaley and Master Dormir approached.

Master Dormir placed his hand on Plock's shoulder. "I will be taking him to the Mages' College."

Kaley waved to Kaste. "I want to talk to you for a moment."

Kaste stayed back while Master Dormir walked off with Plock. He turned to Kaley. "Yeah? What did you want to talk about?"

"I don't know much about magic, but I've known you and Plock for a few years now—and I'm trusting that you told the truth. Don't betray that trust," Kaley said.

Kaste let out a deep sigh and spoke with a heavy heart. "Thank you. I am right about this. I'll stake my future on it."

"That's comforting to hear." Kaley gave Kaste a hug and whispered into his ear. "Don't screw this chance up."

"Pack your things!" Dorak shouted toward Tarkas's room as he approached.

Tarkas got out of bed and rubbed his neck. He looked out the small window—it was dark outside. "Can this wait until morning? Why do we have to head out now?"

"Because Zara needs to get to the elf kingdom now—so we can end her life sooner," Dorak said.

Tarkas rolled his eyes and lay back down on the bed. "We'll wait until morning. No one's traveling in the dark. And if Zara tries to attack, it'll be harder to see her at night. Let's wait with the rest of the group."

Dorak grunted. "You always did think logically. Fine—but we leave at dawn!"

Tarkas groaned. "Ugh, I didn't need this."

The Final Battle

"Komuhiok." Kal woke up with Kleo by his side; he kissed her on the lips. "Come with me."

"Come with you? I have a job here; I can't just leave," Kleo said.

"Marry me, and then you won't have a job anymore," Kal pleaded. "I don't know when. We'll be back here after today, and I want you to come with me."

"How can you afford me?" She looked at him with sad eyes. "I would love to go with you to Kelonia, but I barely know you, and how can you afford me?"

"I'll get a loan from the Queen to show good relations with our kingdoms. When I get back to Centorria, I will have them send the money back here," Kal said.

"Kal, I love the idea of going back to Kelonia and spending more time with you, but it's just not that easy. I will be here whenever you need me."

He kissed her on the lips. "I will come back for you. Stay safe and take care."

She kissed him one more time. "Now you need to go. Travel safe."

"Tarkas, I need to speak with you," Kaste said, walking up to Tarkas, who was helping pack up one of the gryphons.

"He doesn't need to talk to you, mage," Dorak snarled at Kaste.

"Dorak, I can talk to whoever I want." Tarkas stopped fiddling with the bags and gave Kaste his full attention. "What's up?"

"Master Dormir wants you to travel with us. On the way there, we're the ones transporting Zara. I know draining energy is unpleasant for you, but Master Dormir thinks she's the bigger threat. If things go badly—well, you know," Kaste explained.

Tarkas paused for a moment. "It makes me uncomfortable to be around her, but I guess if that's how Master Dormir wants it, I can do that."

"Zara will ride with me on Brimstone," Dorak said, and Brimstone snorted, kicking its foot.

Kaste rolled his eyes. "That's why you're not escorting her. We need to make sure she gets to Kelonia in one piece. So please escort Kellwyn."

Dorak made a fist and growled, but Tarkas placed his hand between them. "No fighting. You'll get your revenge."

"Why are you even coming? Shouldn't you be watching your brother? You got what you wanted," Dorak grunted.

Before Kaste could snap back, Tarkas spoke up. "Hey—he's still our friend and ally. Stop it!"

Dorak took a moment to calm down. "Fine." He went back to packing.

Tarkas left with Kaste to go over to the other gryphon.

"What is Dorak's issue? I thought we were becoming friends?" Kaste asked.

"He's just mad at the whole magic-user thing. Magic users have never been welcome in the village because of past incidents. Now that the mages are trying to group me in with them... we're brothers, and I think making me sound like a magic user creates a divide between us. So don't take it personally. He's hot-headed," Tarkas explained.

They reached the side of the gryphon, and Kaste petted it a bit. "I see. Yeah, I can live with that. Not everyone likes magic users."

Master Dormir soon arrived with Prince Veylin, Guard Solmack, and another mage escorting the prisoners.

"Well, hello, Kaste. I didn't see you this morning," Dormir said.

"I didn't know I was needed. I got up early and headed down here," Kaste replied.

"It would have been useful for you to help transport the prisoners," Dormir said. He waved for the other mage to hand him Zara's shackles. "I need you and Tarkas to escort Zara—together."

Kaste raised an eyebrow. "Are you not coming with us?"

"I'll be taking my horse and going by land. I have other bu—"

Kaste and Zara locked eyes.

"So you're the one I keep hearing about," Zara taunted.

Kaste tightened his grip on the chains and glared back. "I hope it's all about my authority."

"Oh, right. Aren't you the little brother's keeper? How dare he make his own choices or have a life outside of you?" Zara grinned.

Kaste started forming a ball of magic in his other hand. "Is this going to be your attitude the entire trip? Because if so, you won't make it there."

Tarkas interrupted. "Look, it's a long trip. I'm sure we can find something else to talk about."

Zara grinned. "Oh, Tarkas, my sweet nephew. If we weren't related, I'd kiss you." She turned her gaze to Kaste. "Could you kiss him for me?"

Kaste yanked her chains. "Watch your mouth."

"Oh my, the barbarism is starting to rub off on you," Zara said.

"Zara, be lucky you're still alive. I could hand you over to Dorak right now, and you wouldn't make the trip," Tarkas threatened.

She moved her shackles toward Tarkas. "Please, then. Lead the way. I am at your whim."

They were soon all packed up. Dorak, Prince Veylin, and Kellwyn rode on Brimstone. Kaste, Tarkas, and Zara were on the gryphon, while Lira, Kal, and Master Dormir rode on horseback. It was a two-day trip at the speed they were going.

When night came, they found a clearing in the forest to regroup. When the gryphons landed, Kaste handed Zara's chains to Tarkas, jumped off, walked a safe distance away from the group, and let out a loud cry. He then blasted a tree with his magic.

Tarkas handed the chains to Dorak and went to check on him. "Hey, it's okay. She was just trying to get on your nerves. Don't listen to her."

Kaste kicked the ground. "She drives me insane. I can't deal with this."

Tarkas placed a hand on his shoulder. "She bothers me too. But we have a job to do, and it'll be over soon. Don't let her get to you."

Kaste turned and gave Tarkas a hug. "I needed this."

Tarkas hugged him tightly, and their embrace turned into a passionate kiss. They moved toward a nearby tree and began making out. After a few moments, Tarkas stopped when Kaste reached for his belt.

Tarkas pulled back. "We don't have time for this. And it's too soon."

Kaste sighed. "Yeah, I agree. I'm sorry about that."

"Don't worry. It was well received," Tarkas said with a small smile. "But we've got to get back to camp. Think you can handle it?"

"I'll try. Who knows—maybe she'll be dead by the time we get back," Kaste muttered as he headed back.

When they returned, the horses had arrived and the rest of the party was settling in. Zara sat on a rock, unusually quiet, while Dorak glared at her, gripping the rope that bound her hands. Master Dormir walked over to Kaste and Tarkas.

"How was the trip down? Why is Zara with Dorak?"

Kaste rolled his eyes. Tarkas answered. "The trip down was rough, but Zara's safe. Dorak hasn't touched her."

"I see. Well, as long as it's working. But I think we should get to bed so we can leave first thing in the morning," Dormir said.

"What about dinner?" Kal asked. "We've been traveling all day. We need food first."

Lira pulled a cooking pot from her pack. "Yeah. I'll start cooking. But I agree—we need to leave at first light."

Prince Veylin turned to Kal. "Want to help me set up camp?"

"Sure, sounds good to me," Kal replied. "Who's taking first watch?"

Tarkas raised his hand. "I'll take the first watch."

That night, they took turns keeping watch. Dorak kept guard over the prisoner. Tarkas considered speaking with Zara—asking more about who he really was—but ultimately decided against it. She wasn't his family. Dorak was his family. Who was to say they weren't broth-ers?

He lay awake thinking of the life he left behind—the village, being just a non-magical person. He still wondered what was happening to him. This was the most adventure he'd ever experienced. He longed to see his home again, even if it was now just a wasteland.

In the morning, they packed up and continued their journey. Kaste walked over to Dorak.

"Can you take Zara today? I don't think I can finish the trip with her."

Dormir stepped forward. "I don't see a problem with that arrange-ment."

Kaste clenched his fists and rolled his eyes. "She irritated and ha-rassed me non-stop yesterday. I'm not going through that again."

"I didn't kill her last night, as much as I wanted to," Dorak mut-tered. "But I do know how to respect other laws. I just hoped mine had more authority, since it happened first."

Dormir sighed. "You win this one, Kaste. You can ride with Kell-wyn instead."

Lira spoke up. "Why is it so important who rides with who? I thought this was just about Dorak being unstable."

Master Dormir sighed again. "I just like things to be in a certain order. I don't like to change the plan, that's all."

Kaste raised an eyebrow. "No you didn't. I know you too well. You had a plan—and I want to know what it is."

Master Dormir let out a sigh. "If you must know, I wanted to see you speak up for yourself. That's all. And I'm glad you did—you were getting a bit gloomy the last few days, and I wanted to see the fight back in your eyes."

"Oh, you senile old man!" Kaste raised his fist, and a red ball of magic formed in his hand.

Tarkas grabbed Kaste's arm. "Not now. Don't fight your allies."

Kaste extinguished the magic and turned to Tarkas. "Sorry—I'm just a little on edge."

"I know. But we need to get going while there's still daylight. If we leave now, we'll make it to the city by nightfall," Tarkas said.

They all finished packing up the beasts and began their journey toward the city.

Just as they had planned, they reached the gates of Kelonia at nightfall. It was getting dark, but there was still a sliver of daylight left.

"It's late. Do you think the queen will be awake?" Lira asked.

"If she's not, she will be for this. Let's get going," Kaley said, kicking her horse into motion and rushing through the city.

"I thought animals weren't allowed past the city gates?" Kal said.

"From what I'm gathering, Kaley is making an exception," Prince Veylin replied, and Dorak rode Brimstone through the city. The rest followed Kaley's path.

When they reached the palace gates, they dismounted. Kaley, now fully in command mode, got off her horse.

"All right, bring the prisoners and follow me," she said, heading toward the palace. "Kal, come with me and stay close."

They entered together, Kaley leading the way through the palace. She spotted one of the guards.

"Kith! Go get the queen—she's needed, and it cannot wait!" she barked.

"Right away, Captain!" he replied, rushing off toward the queen's chambers.

Kaley led everyone up the stairs to the throne room. She grabbed each prisoner by the shoulder and threw them down in front of the throne.

"Kneel before the queen."

Zara and Kellwyn obeyed, kneeling with their hands retied behind their backs.

"Now stay there and wait for the queen."

They all waited a few tense moments in silence, Kaley's commanding presence filling the room. Then Queen Keltrice entered, walking down the hall in her best dressing gown.

"Kaley, I was just getting ready for bed. This had better be good. Sorry—you'll have to excuse my appearance."

"It is, Your Majesty," Captain Kaley said, bowing slightly. "I bring you the traitors—and have returned our temple's sacred orb. We got here as soon as we could."

Keltrice looked down at the two kneeling figures. "I thought there were five who attacked the temple. Where are the others?"

Kaley hesitated for a moment, then pointed with her boot. "This one here is the ringleader, the one who organized the attack. And this one is a follower of Marion. They're the important ones. One is still at large, and the others... are no longer with us."

Keltrice narrowed her eyes. "A Marionite? Now *that* is serious. You've done well, Captain."

Dorak stepped forward and pointed at Zara. "This one is also wanted among my people. You can have the other—but I want *her* to be punished by my tribe's laws."

"Punished by your people's laws?" Keltrice looked sharply at Dorak. "You're from the Crystal Caves, aren't you? From what I remember, your people were peaceful. How exactly would you go about punishing her?"

"We were peaceful. And her punishment would be death by my axe, since I am the new chief—she attacked my village, committing genocide against my people," Dorak said.

Keltrice paused for a moment. "It is late. I will consider your request and give you an answer in the morning when we decide both their punishments."

Dorak grunted, displeased with the delay, but understood he was a guest in this kingdom. "Understood. I will await your decision."

"Guards, take the prisoners to the dungeon." Keltrice looked at Kal. "Prince Kal, is it? Nice to see you again. We'll talk in the morning." She stood up from her throne and returned to her bedchamber.

"Now what?" Lyra asked, looking around the darkening halls.

Kaley paused for a moment. "I guess... we go to bed."

"Yes, but *you* have a place here. What about the rest of us?" Lyra added.

Kaley nodded slowly. "There are some extra beds in the barracks. You could stay there tonight, if you want. Follow me."

They all followed Kaley down to the barracks. When they arrived, they found most of the beds were taken—except for two. Kaley spotted one of the other guards.

"What's going on with the barracks? This area *always* has beds," she asked, clearly irritated.

The guard responded. "Oh, Captain—while you were gone, the queen brought in some new recruits. The barracks are full."

Kaley turned to the group, annoyed. "We've got two beds. I have my own room, so I'm not worried—but I want to make sure you're all comfortable."

The beds were small, barely enough for one person, let alone someone Dorak or Tarkas's size.

"I'll take a bed," Kal said.

Prince Veylin nodded. "I'll take the other, if people are okay with that."

Kaste spoke up. "Is there an inn nearby?"

Kaley nodded. "Yeah, there's one not far from here, if you prefer. I can give you directions."

"Then... I'd prefer that. I'll meet you in the morning. Anyone who'd like to come with me is welcome," Kaste said.

"You'll find me in the stables," Dorak added.

"I'll follow you, Kaste," Tarkas said. "What about you, Lyra?"

Lyra's face turned bright red. "I was going to stay with Kaley. We talked about it before we left—I could stay with her."

Kaste shrugged. "Alright then. We'll meet back here in the morning."

Kaste lay in the bed next to Tarkas. They lay there beside each other—sleepless, contactless. Kaste let out a heavy sigh.

"If you sigh any louder, I won't be the only one who can't sleep.
What's on your mind?" Tarkas rolled over to face him.

"I'm tired of all of this," Kaste said. "And I'm worried about what
Master Dormir has planned for me. I *know* he's planning something,
and I worry about what's next for me, then." He paused. "Things are
changing. I just wanted my brother back."

Tarkas let out a sigh. "I see. Yeah, there's a lot about to change. I'm
almost worried about what's going to happen next. It feels so close to
being over—but that feels too good to be true. You can leave if you
want to. I won't tell Dormir."

Kaste shook his head. "I want to see this through. Hey, if tomorrow
is the last day, and your people are avenged—what's next for you?"

Tarkas lay on his back, staring at the ceiling, pondering. "I don't
know. Winter's near, so I'll need a place to stay, but I don't have any
plans. Skolsav said I'd be welcome in his village, but... knowing what
I know about myself, I'm curious—curious to go back to my village,
maybe see the gods and talk to them. I don't know."

"Do any of these plans potentially involve me?" Kaste asked.

Tarkas turned toward Kaste. "I, uh... didn't think about it. I
thought you wanted to be with your brother. We're only sharing a bed
right now because it was cheaper. But... do you want me?"

Kaste sighed. "I don't know. If you still need time, I understand. But I want you to know—if you ever want to visit, you have a place with me."

"Thank you for that offer," Tarkas said after a pause. "Are you getting any power boost from me now?"

Kaste paused for a moment, closed his eyes, then opened them again. "Not much, if anything. Why are you asking?"

"Because part of me wants to be close to you, but I don't want it to be about power. I *can* give you a power boost."

Tarkas rolled onto his side and smiled at Kaste. "Thank you. That means a lot to me, because I don't know if there's a place where I even belong anymore. I don't know what's expected of me when this is over."

"You're the son of your gods. Have you thought about going to them? Talking to them about all this?" Kaste asked.

Tarkas's heart dropped—like a brick wall of realization had hit him. "I never thought of it. My family *was* my tribe, and they were the gods. But like I said before... it feels like I died and woke up in a totally different world. The gods weren't cursed people living forever—and I wasn't one of them. My tribe was still alive. I had never seen a city the size of this. I don't know if I *want* to talk to them. I just want things to go back to the way they were. I want to go back to tribal life."

"Have you talked to Dorak about this?" Kaste asked.

Tarkas groaned. "I tried, but he's too goal-focused. I think this is really hard on him too, and staying focused is how he's coping. So when this is done... I don't know what will happen. It'll end, and we'll figure things out from there."

Kaste leaned in and gave Tarkas a kiss on the lips. "Don't radiate magic. I want to be with the *real* Tarkas—if you're ready."

Tarkas paused for a moment, but he could see the sincerity in Kaste's eyes. "I'd like that. But let's just stay close tonight."

Morning came. The judgment of Zara was upon them.

They all gathered in the throne room after breakfast. Dorak stood poised, ready for the negotiations to begin. Queen Keltrice and Kal walked down the hall together. All they could hear from their conversation was her saying:

"No. When this ordeal is done, you are to stay here as a prince. That is final."

Kal didn't look pleased.

The queen sat on her throne, and they all bowed.

"Kellwyn will stay here, be questioned, and—in time—executed for his crimes. But first, he will lead us to the rest of the Marionites. Captain Kaley, you'll be in charge of that."

She turned to the rest of the group. "As for Zara... Dorak, would you be willing to execute her here in our kingdom? She appears, as you say, too dangerous to live—but she is as much a criminal here as she is to your people."

Dorak grunted in approval. "My homeland lies in ruin because of that witch. I have no problem ending her on your grounds, Your Highness."

Queen Keltrice grinned. "Good. Then we will proceed with the execution. Captain Kaley, please see to the arrangements." The queen rose from her throne and headed down the hall.

Tarkas raised an eyebrow at Kaste. "That was quick."

Kaste stood up. "Monarchs don't have time for deliberation—they like to make quick decisions. I want to go find Master Dormir."

Kaste and Tarkas made their way to the ruined temple, where they suspected Dormir was investigating. They walked past the training grounds and the judgment zone where the execution was to be held.

"We'll be back for this," Kaste said. "I have a feeling you're going to want to see it."

Tarkas sighed. "As much as I don't enjoy the sight of bloodshed, I feel a responsibility to be there for this one."

They continued on to the ruined temple where the attack had taken place during their first visit to the city. They saw priests repairing the structure.

Kaste approached one of the workers. "Is Master Dormir here? Tall, white-bearded human?"

The priest looked up and pointed. "He went to the basement."

Kaste and Tarkas descended into the temple basement, wandering through a few corridors until they found Master Dormir examining some books.

"Fascinating. All this magic—I've never seen anything like it. I had no idea the Veylin had discovered so much," Dormir said. Then, as if sensing their presence, he lifted his head. "Oh, hello there, Kaste, Tarkas. What brings you here?"

Kaste spoke. "We came to find you. Zara is going to be executed today."

Master Dormir let out a long, thoughtful sigh. "I think that's for the best. So—have you charged the battle axe? Or are you shooting her with one of your arrows?"

Tarkas frowned. "What are you talking about?"

Master Dormir pulled a red tome off the shelf and opened it. "Dorak's battle-axe and your bow are made from the petrified wood of the Tree of Life. When charged with magic, it can cut and destroy anything. Did no one explain that when you received those items? Zara knows. The only way to charge them is with a conduit. You didn't know any of this?"

Tarkas's eyes widened. "I was dead when Dorak got them. No one told me. How is there even a book on this? I didn't even know I *was* a conduit until you told me!"

"Well, I had to *find* this book—it's been missing from our library for many years. I'm glad I finally located it. That's why I told you and Kaste to stay near each other. If a fight breaks out, we'll need Tarkas to charge the axe, the bow, and Kaste. Most wizards can't handle a full charge, but from what I've seen, Kaste is... different," Master Dormir said.

Kaste clenched his fists. "You're telling me this *now*, old man? You always give me half the story! You never think it's important to tell me anything *in advance*!"

"I wanted to see how long it would take you to figure things out. You only get one true opportunity to *learn* knowledge—and I'd rather you find it on your own," Master Dormir explained.

Just then, bells began to ring throughout the city, and he smiled.

Tarkas felt a sinking sensation in his stomach. "The execution—we need to go."

Tarkas and Kaste bolted from the temple and made their way to the judgment zone. As they arrived, they saw Dorak raising his axe, Zara kneeling with her neck bare on the chopping block.

Tarkas cried out. "Stop!"—but it was too late.

The axe came down—but instead of striking, a forcefield of magic shimmered around Zara's neck. She levitated into the air.

"Foolish barbarian," she hissed. "You thought I'd let you kill me that easily?"

The sky turned grey. A storm swirled to life, just like during their first encounter. Lightning cracked through the clouds as Airis appeared, riding his undead steed, hurling bolts of lightning toward Kaste.

"Look out!" a voice cried.

Lightning forked overhead like claws. Tarkas shoved Kaste aside and drew back his bow. Above the executioner's stage, Airis hurled jagged lances of lighting from a darkened sky. Dorak's axe came down heavy and true toward Zara, but her force-field bloomed violet around her as she laughed viciously.

Tarkas sprinted for the scaffold where Dorak and Zara's duel cracked the air like thunder. He loosed an arrow mid-run; the shaft punched into Airis's undead steed, throwing the sorcerer to the ground.

Chaos spilled across the square. Kaley drew her sword and prepared to fight any and all enemies; Kal and Prince Veylin met a sudden rush of hidden foes from the arcades.

Airis staggered up into Kaste's path, helm tilting, voice a curl of venom. "So—you're my replacement. Tarkas is mine."

Kaste's staff lifted, runes sparking. "Jealousy doesn't look good on you."

Words ended. Magic spoke—fire and shadow colliding in teeth-rattling bursts that threw sparks across the wet stone.

Tarkas shouldered through the hiss of falling lightning, eyes on Dorak. Zara floated just above the block, smile sharp as glass. "So," she purred. "you've finally learned to use what you are. You could still join me, nephew."

"Not a chance," Tarkas growled.

Dorak drew back for the killing stroke. Tarkas caught the haft of the axe. The axe's petrified-wood haft thrummed through his palm, glowing with a magical charge.

"What are you doing?" Dorak barked.

"Charging it," Tarkas said.

Power seared along its grain.

"I don't like this," Dorak snarled. "You're not a magic user."

"It doesn't matter. If we want her dead, this is how." Tarkas said, nocking another arrow.

The engravings along the blade ignited. Dorak roared and swung. The charged edge met Zara's ward and shattered it. A noise like a thousand distant screams filled the air as scattered shards of magical energy spilled into the wind and melted away. For the first time in a thousand years, something like fear flickered in her eyes.

"Oh," she breathed. "Now this is interesting." Her aura flared; power doubled, she lashed out with a blade of ethereal force.

Across the square, Kaste and Airis fought each other, bolts and counters strobing. A lance of blue energy caught Kaste high in the shoulder, burning through cloth and skin. Tarkas saw the hit, snapped a shot; his arrow winged Airis, slowing him but not stopping him.

Tarkas vaulted from the stage, bow already drawn, a charged arrow sighted on the sorcerer's heart. He loosed—Airis twisted and flipped across the stones, a pretty trick across the stones. Tarkas hit hard, breath blasted from his lungs.

Airis loomed, predatory smile behind wet steel. "Come with me," he said, hand extended. "The game's over. My love."

Pain and betrayal surged up like floodwater—Airis's faked death, the lies, the ruin he'd left behind. Tarkas took the offered hand—not to rise, but to pull.

He drained.

It wasn't theft so much as untying a knot. Magic and life bucked through him, ugly and hot. Airis gasped, tried to wrench free. "What—what are you—"

"Ending this," Tarkas said through his teeth.

Airis yanked, but Tarkas's grip held. Flesh shriveled under Tarkas's fingers; the elegant gauntlet sagged on a hand gone claw-thin, parchment over bone. Horror flashed through Tarkas. He let go.

Airis stared at the ruin of his own wrist. "What did you?" His voice shook, equal parts rage and disbelief. "Why, would you do this to me?"

"If you can't be trusted with power," Tarkas said, cold as rain. "You don't get to keep it."

Airis tried to conjure. A fire-orb swelled and died in smoke. He tried again—smaller, meaner—panic rising. "What did you do to me, Tarkas?!"

"You did it to yourself."

A furious whistle tore from Airis. The undead steed clawed up from the slick stones. He vaulted to the saddle and bolted from the colonnade and rode into the air, but Tarkas's last arrow followed. It struck; Airis toppled, vanished past the walls of the city, a shadowy specter swallowed by deeper shadow.

On the stage, Dorak and Zara crashed together again. Zara swung her blade of pure light from the air. "Centuries since I've had a fight like this," she snarled. "You cannot hope to—"

"You murdered my people," Dorak said, eyes lit from within. "You end here."

They traded blows—steel on sorcery, charged edge chewing her defenses to ribbons. Dorak knocked her guard wide and set his boots.

"I am Dorak son of Gorak, chief of the protectors of the Crystal Caves," he roared, "and you pay for what you wrought."

He raised the glowing axe and brought it down in one clean, merciless arc.

The blade went into her chest.

For an instant the force that had pretended to be immortality clung to the body like mist—and then it unraveled, thin as breath. The head struck wood; the body folded with strange, quiet grace. The storm, at last, remembered how to fade. "I lived... over a thousand years... cursed with immortality," Zara whispered. "And now—this... this is what it feels like... to die." The light went out of her eyes. The thread snapped. Rain hissed where it touched the still-warm blade.

No one cheered. Dorak lowered the axe, shoulders heaving, and bowed his head—not to her, but to the dead who could not return. Tarkas felt Kaste's fingers find his, steady despite the burn on his shoulder. Across the broken colonnade, Captain Kaley eased but did not break.

Queen Keltrice stepped forward, voice carrying like a bell through the damp. "Justice is done," she said. "See the body sealed, the wards restored. Our city will not cradle the remnant of this storm."

Dorak looked to Tarkas—something gentler in the iron of his face. "Brother," he said, rough with rain and relief. "It's finished."

"So it is," Tarkas murmured, eyes on the horizon where Airis had vanished, his ruined hand a memory Tarkas could still feel. "There will be echoes."

"Then we'll answer them," Dorak said. He glanced once at the block, at the place where a thousand-year curse had finally learned how to end, and turned toward the palace lights, where reckoning and the long work after victory waited.

Epilogue

Dorak sat on the edge of the narrow barracks bed, the axe across his knees and the smell of oiled wood in the quiet. Rain ticked at the shutters. Somewhere down the corridor a watchman cleared his throat, and the sound went thin and small against the kind of silence that follows storms.

A year ago, he had known his life: the Crystal Caves, the rhythm of guard shifts and harvest feasts, the old songs his mother hummed. A year ago he had known his gods, too—known what they asked, what they promised, how a man kept faith.

Now he knew didn't know what to feel.

He grunted once, the sound half laugh, half refusal. Satisfaction sat in him like a stone—cool, heavy, unarguable. He had honoured the dead. He had cut the cord that bound their ghosts to a name they feared. He had taken Zara's head with his own hands and given his people the only justice left in a world that had not kept them safe.

No remorse lived in the place where the stroke had landed. Only the question that came afterward, the one vengeance never answers: what now.

There was no going home. The Caves were ruin and ash; their meanings scattered like blown snow. Chief of what, then? Protector of whom? A title without a hearth is a blade without a haft; there was no land or people left to rule.

He ran his thumb along the old runes in the axe's haft. The charge had gone out of it hours ago, leaving behind the memory of heat—a phantom pulse in the grain. He remembered the feel of Tarkas's hand on the wood, the way power had climbed the rings and lit the edge from within. Brother, he had said, and meant it.

His thoughts strayed to the gods, and he let them. The stories he'd been fed in the dark of the cavern halls had cracked in the light of the world above. Maybe that was a kind of mercy. Men could stand up straighter when the ceilings lifted.

Zara was gone. That mattered. The square would be sanded and scrubbed by morning, and still some part of the city would remember, the way stone remembers the shape of the river that carved it. Airis had slunk into the drains with a ruined hand and a new debt. There would be echoes, as the mage had said. Let them come.

The hollowness wasn't grief. It was a room emptied for something else but not yet filled. He listened to it and did not flinch.

"Finished," he said aloud, to the axe, to the dark, to the ones who might still be listening. "Finished here."

He stood. His shoulders felt lighter and older at once. When morning came he would walk to the queen and ask for maps, for names of scattered families, for stonecutters and masons and a wagon of seed grain. If the Crystal Caves were gone, then the Crystal People would not be. You could build walls in a new place. You could teach children a song anywhere there was a fire.

For tonight, he sat back down and let the rain count the breaths for him. He closed his eyes and, for the first time since the caves fell, allowed himself to imagine a future that did not begin with a blade.

Tarkas cinched the last strap on his pack and checked the bowstring with a thumb. The room still smelled of oil and wet wool. Kaste leaned in the doorway, hands tucked into his sleeves, watching him with a tired half-smile.

"So," Kaste said, light but not careless, "where are you off to next?"

Tarkas shouldered the pack and met his eye. "Could ask you the same."

Kaste huffed a breath. "Family first. There's... winter work to do. My brother won't mend himself, and the court will want answers I can't keep dodging. I'll spend the cold months making sure he doesn't fall apart—and sorting the pieces Dormir left on my desk."

Tarkas nodded. "Good. You love him. You've carried enough to earn a quieter season."

He glanced toward the shutter, where a thin wash of gray promised morning. "I'm thinking north. Skolsav's village—the Molav marsh. If Zara left any knives in the reeds, they'll rattle there. And if not... his people are the closest thing to a home I can find before the snows. Better to winter with a tribe that knows the land." He paused, then added, softer. "Everything else is gone. I can't pretend the old paths are still there."

Kaste crossed the room and pulled him into an embrace that was firm and brief and said more than either of them wanted to say badly. "If you ever need a roof, you have mine," he murmured. "I know I'm untangling a mess, and this year chewed us both raw, but—what we have isn't a battlefield accident. It's real."

Tarkas pressed his brow to Kaste's for a heartbeat and let the quiet settle. "I felt it too," he said. "Not since Aerith." He drew back, searching Kaste's face. "I'm glad we had the time we did. But right now, you're the wizard with a tower of books and a family to set in order. And I'm... I'm the man who needs the road and a tree line to tell him who he is. Cities make me itch. I have to go find the place my name fits."

Kaste's mouth tilted. "Then go find it." He reached to Tarkas's bracer and, after a moment of hesitation, tied a thin strip of red-dyed cord around the leather—a simple ward, a simple promise. "For luck. And so I'll worry a little less."

Tarkas's rough fingers brushed Kaste's knuckles. "I'll keep it." He stepped back, the pack settling into its proper place on his shoulders. "Maybe one day the road runs me past your door again."

"It will," Kaste said, no bravado in it, only faith. "Paths like ours cross. That's what roads are for."

They held each other's gaze one last moment, and then the spell broke. Tarkas touched the cord once more, turned toward the hall, and the two of them let go without dragging the goodbye out so long it hurt.

"I'll see you in the spring," Kaste called after him.

Tarkas glanced back over his shoulder. "I'm sure you will," he said. "This isn't the end of anything." He lifted a hand in a small salute and was gone into the grey morning.

The stables smelled of hay and damp leather. Gryphons shifted in their stalls, bronze eyes blinking as Kaley and Lira tightened cinches and checked buckles by lantern light.

Bootsteps in the aisle. Kal appeared in a new traveling coat the color of old wine, a lute slung awkwardly over one shoulder.

Kaley didn't look up from her work. "Oh, no, you don't. Where do you think you're going?"

Kal lifted the lute a fraction, like a flag of truce. "Alwyndia," he said. "To see my girlfriend, Kleo. And to see what being... normal feels like for a winter."

Kaley finally looked, one brow climbing. "You're still seeing that prostitute?"

"Yes," he said, without flinching. "I don't know if it lasts. We grew up cut off from who we were supposed to be; we understand each other. I want to see where it goes. And I don't want to support her as the prince I'm not anymore. I want to support her as a person. So." He patted the lute. "I'll play."

Lira snorted, warm and incredulous. "Do you even know how to play the lute?"

Kal rubbed the back of his neck. "Well... sort of. I mean, it can't be that hard. Seven strings, seven days of the week. I learn a string a day. By next market I'm a minstrel."

"That's not how strings or weeks work," Kaley said dryly. She stepped over, caught his left hand, and set his fingers along the fretboard. "Start here. Press until it hurts, then lighter. Breathe."

Kal tried. The first chord came out like a chair breaking.

A gryphon down the row rattled its beak against the stall in protest. Lira laughed outright. "Hero of the temple," she said. "Bane of tuning pegs."

Kal grinned despite himself and adjusted his grip. "I'll get the hang of it."

"Someday," Lira said, eyes bright.

Kal dipped his head to them both. "Thank you. For everything."

"Write," Kaley said.

"And practice," Lira added. "Preferably far from nervous animals."

"I'll try to do both," he said. He took a breath, squared his shoulders, and turned toward the yard where the morning was going pale. "Seven strings," he murmured, half to himself. "Seven days."

The stables rang with easy laughter at the thought of Kal—once a prince of Centorria—trying on the life of a bard. He only grinned, shouldered his pack, took up his lute, and set off to fetch his horse for the road back to Alwyndia.

A little later, Kaley and Lira were tightening saddles on their gryphons when Kaste came down the aisle, travel cloak half-fastened.

"So," he asked Kaley, "what did you decide?"

"Plants," Kaley said, giving a final tug on a cinch. "Herbalism, midwives' gardens—the practical side. If we're taking Lira to Merleinland, I want to learn from the healers there."

Lira smoothed a hand over the gryphon's neck. "We're going to the coastal ward, to speak with the sea-temple midwives. Books only go so far. I want answers about the baby—and about how to bring a child safely into this world."

Kaste's smile softened. "That sounds right. If you want to stay in touch—I'll be at my house this winter, gods willing. If the College drags me back, leave a note at the gate. I need time with my brother. We've both earned it."

He'd barely finished when a familiar voice floated in from the doorway. "Kaste."

Master Dormir stood there, cloak beaded with rain, eyes keen despite the yawn he tried—and failed—to hide.

Kaste straightened. "Master. What did you want to talk about?"

"Where you're headed."

"I'll collect my brother from the Mages' College," Kaste said, "then home. I'd like—just for a season—to get back to what we were."

Dormir's brows knit. "After a year like this? You've learned things most scholars spend three lifetimes failing to touch, and you'd shelve them to mind your brother?"

"He's my brother," Kaste said, jaw tight. "Of course I would."

Dormir exhaled, a sound edged with age. "Listen to me: you've stumbled into living currents. Tarkas's conduit nature, the petrified-wood relics, the... unusual circumstances of Lira's child. They all deserve study. You deserve to study them. Come back, not as my pupil under a tangle of rules, but to continue the work."

Kaste folded his arms. "At the College, you tied my hands. You made everything harder than it had to be."

"I was harder than I had to be," Dormir said. "I saw a younger version of myself and mistook harshness for guidance. I'm tired of that mistake. I'm retiring soon, Kaste. I want someone I trust to pick up the threads I've guarded too long. You're the first person in years I can speak to plainly about any of this."

Kaley and Lira had gone very still, leather creaking softly under their fingers.

Kaste glanced between them, then back to Dormir. "You're asking me to return."

"I'm asking you to continue," Dormir said. "Bring your brother home. See him safe. Then come back and set terms that let you do the work as it needs doing."

Kaste hesitated long enough for the gryphon to huff and stamp, then nodded once. "All right. I'll go with you. We'll put the terms in writing when we arrive."

Dormir's shoulders eased. "That is all I ask. Thank you."

Kaley clapped Kaste's shoulder, approval in the press of her hand. Lira's fingers threaded briefly through his, warm and grateful.

"Go fetch your brother," Lira said. "We'll bring back what the midwives know."

"And we'll all meet in the spring," Kaley added, swinging into her saddle. "With better answers than we have today."

Kaste managed a crooked smile. "Spring it is."

Outside, the yard brightened with a thin, winter sun. The gryphons shook out their wings. Plans settled like saddles into place, and the road—several roads—waited.

Tarkas found Dorak where the light from the barracks window made a dull square on the floor. The axe leaned against the wall within reach. Dorak didn't rise when Tarkas stepped in; he lifted his eyes, that was all.

"Got any plans?" Tarkas asked.

A grunt. "You look like you do."

"Winter's coming," Tarkas said. "I don't much fancy stone walls or court dinners. Skolsav's village sits up in the Molav marsh. He offered us a place if we needed one. Says his folk live a lot like we did—more fish, less stone. It's the closest thing to home I can find before the snow."

Dorak's mouth twitched. "Better than this city." He pushed a breath through his nose. "Worth a try. For the winter."

Tarkas nodded, then stood there a moment longer, words settling into the right order. "Listen. You've been there my whole life. Brother. Family. The Caves are gone. The gods aren't what we thought. Our village is ash. I don't know what any of that makes us now. I only know the cold's coming and we don't have much laid by. We try the marsh. We see."

"I'm not arguing," Dorak said, dry as flint.

Tarkas scoffed. "Good. Because the truth is, I'm... wrong-footed. The last year turned everything sideways. I died and woke to a world I didn't recognize. You dragged me back, and you stayed. Thank you for both. But I think we need to learn—again—who we are. Not what we were told."

Dorak rose and took up the axe. "You're right. We'll go to these Molav swamps and see what comes."

Tarkas's shoulders eased. "Thank you for being reasonable."

"Don't say anything about it," Dorak said. "You'll ruin my reputation."

The two men laughed and hefted their packs. The grey skies thundered once as they turned toward the gate. It was a hard enough world to find peace in, even before their home was destroyed. But there was still peace to be had in it, surely if they only wandered far enough.

There was nothing else to do, now, but start walking.

www.ingramcontent.com/pod-product-compliance
Lightning Source LLC
Chambersburg PA
CBHW051515170626
46811CB00002B/838